Rex St

REX STOUT, the creator of Neiv woile, was born in
Noblesville, Indiana, in 1886, the sixth of nine children
of John and Lucetta Todhunter Stout, both Quakers.
Shortly after his birth, the family moved to Wakarusa,
Kansas. He was educated in a country school, but by the
age of nine he was recognized throughout the state as a
prodigy in arithmetic. Mr. Stout briefly attended the
University of Kansas, but left to enlist in the Navy, and
spent the next two years as a warrant officer on board
President Theodore Roosevelt's yacht. When he left the
Navy in 1908, Rex Stout began to write free-lance
articles and worked as a sightseeing guide and as an
itinerant bookkeeper. Later he devised and implemented
a school banking system which was installed in four
hundred cities and towns throughout the country. In 1927
Mr. Stout retired from the world of finance and, with the
proceeds of his banking scheme, left for Paris to write
serious fiction. He wrote three novels that received
favorable reviews before turning to detective fiction. His
first Nero Wolfe novel, *Fer-de-Lance*, appeared in 1934.
It was followed by many others, among them *Too Many
Cooks, The Silent Speaker, If Death Ever Slept, The
Doorbell Rang*, and *Please Pass the Guilt*, which established Nero Wolfe as a leading character on a par with
Erle Stanley Gardner's famous protagonist, Perry Ma-
son. During World War II, Rex Stout waged a personal
campaign against Nazism as chairman of the War Writers' Board, master of ceremonies of the radio program
"Speaking of Liberty," and member of several national
committees. After the war he turned his attention to
mobilizing public opinion against the wartime use of
thermonuclear devices, was an active leader in the
Authors' Guild, and resumed writing his Nero Wolfe
novels. Rex Stout died in 1975 at the age of eighty-eight.
A month before his death, he published his seventy-
second Nero Wolfe mystery, *A Family Affair*. Ten years
later, a seventy-third Nero Wolfe mystery was discovered and published in *Death Times Three*.

The Rex Stout Library

REX STOUT

Where There's A Will

Introduction
by Dean R. Koontz

BANTAM BOOKS
NEW YORK · TORONTO · LONDON · SYDNEY · AUCKLAND

A NERO WOLFE MYSTERY

WHERE THERE'S A WILL

A Bantam Crime Line Book / published by arrangement with
the estate of the author

PUBLISHING HISTORY
Farrar & Rinehart edition published 1940
Bantam edition / March 1992

Grateful acknowledgment is made for permission to reproduce the
original cover artwork from the Avon edition of Where There's a
Will. Reprinted by permission of Avon Books.

CRIME LINE and the portrayal of a boxed "cl" are trademarks
of Bantam Books, a division of Bantam Doubleday Dell Publishing Group, Inc.

ISBN 978-0-553-76301-0

Published simultaneously in the United States and Canada

Bantam Books are published by Bantam Books, a division of Bantam Doubleday Dell Publishing Group, Inc. Its trademark, consisting of the words
"Bantam Books" and the portrayal of a rooster, is Registered in U.S. Patent
and Trademark Office and in other countries. Marca Registrada. Bantam
Books, New York, New York.

Introduction

A writer is influenced by everything he reads. Everything. That means not only novels and short stories but newspapers and magazines and cereal boxes and even—God, spare us—the inscrutable scribblings of politicians. If a writer's dog drags home a wad of old paper which is unappetizing to the human eye but on which the mutt has chewed and slobbered with enthusiasm, the writer will be influenced by whatever he reads between the tooth holes and saliva tracks. Although his conscious mind may be easily bored, his subconscious is a perpetually wonderstruck infant that will find a wealth of fascinating data to store away from that dog-gnawed paper.

Aware that the subconscious is a cosmic sponge, writers are often willing to experience anything in the interest of finding material. They will sail to Burma on a freighter to participate in a yak-heaving contest, subject themselves to a survival trek in the Amazon rain forest where they must eat grub pâté to escape starvation, have the inner rims of their nostrils decorated by a carnival tattoo artist at a county fairgrounds in Alabama, and even watch Phil Donahue—all in the hope that the subconscious will mull over these adventures, discover aspects and achieve insights beyond the perceptive ability of the conscious mind, and generate brilliant ideas for novels or short stories.

Some of these writers, with tiny tattooed flames blazing from their nostrils and their shoulders aching from heaving one yak too many and bits of grubs still stuck between their teeth, will react with horror to the suggestion that they might want to *read* as broadly as they travel. If one of these scribblers considers himself a "literary" writer, he doesn't want to contaminate his subconscious mind with an awareness of the styles and prose rhythms of "popular" writers, for fear he might wind up writing a novel that has relevance beyond the insular world of the self-appointed literati or that, God forfend, even has a plot. If he is a science-fiction writer, he may read science fiction to the exclusion of all other forms, convinced that any tale of genetically engineered, brain-eating, laser-toting, cyberpunk aliens with a psychotic need to conquer the universe is certain to be more intellectually stimulating than any story to be found in lesser genres. Some popular writers will not read literary types, partly as a payback for the undeserved insults they have received from those artistes. Some mystery writers will read only mysteries, some Western writers only Westerns, some historical novelists only historicals.

One novelist I've encountered is reluctant to read *any* novels other than his own, for fear of polluting his creative tidepool. If he reads John D. MacDonald,

Philip Roth, Charles Dickens, or anyone else, isn't it possible (he worries) that he will then call forth his own muse only to discover that she is a hideous mutant, twisted beyond all recognition by contamination with those *other* writers? He apparently functions under the impression that his talent came with an engraved-in-stone stylesheet of prodigious specificity, a gift from God that has acquired no patina from life, and that he would have written precisely the same stories when he was two weeks old as he writes now, if only his fingers had been big enough to deal with a typewriter at that tender age.

When it comes to reading fiction, I am an omnivore, largely because I love to read but also because I fear that reading *sparely* will result in my writing being shaped by too narrow a range of influences. Unlike the skittish writer in the previous paragraph, I think that by reading everything, I water down the influence of any one writer and thereby preserve my natural voice. For all of my adult life, I have devoured both popular and "serious" fiction, love stories and science fiction, Westerns and horror novels, tales of academic angst and animal stories, stream-of-consciousness self-indulgence and clockwork-mechanism mystery novels, Jim Harrison and Jim Thompson, John LeCarre and John Barth, Philip K. Dick and Philip Roth and Philip Jose Farmer, though I find the recent work of the middle Philip too Philippic.

I have learned a great deal from an omnivorous literary diet, but two lessons in particular apply to this introduction. First, the very best examples of writing from any genre are equal in quality to the best examples from any other genre, and the finest popular fiction is equal to the finest "serious" fiction. The fragmentation of fiction into genres was largely a marketing ploy of modern publishing. Likewise, the division between popular and serious work was a scheme perpetrated by academics in need of creating a false pantheon of living writers when it became impossible to come up with fresh dissertation topics (to earn degrees and prestige) concerning the writers in the true pantheon, who had been analyzed to exhaustion. Second, the more widely a writer reads, the more he learns about craft and technique, and the more interesting and flavorful his style becomes, just as a vegetable soup becomes more interesting with a multitude of vegetables than it is with only, say, lima beans and broccoli.

Twenty years ago, when I was struggling to find my own voice as a writer, I was reading five novels a week in addition to putting in full days at the typewriter. (We didn't have the great blessing of computers and word-processing software back then. But we didn't have freeway shootouts or Donald Trump, either, so it wasn't altogether a less appealing era.) It was exciting to "discover" a great writer like John D. MacDonald, who had a backlist, and read one book after the other to the point of intoxication. Or Donald Westlake. Hammond Innes. Irwin Shaw. John P. Marquand, who wrote the Pulitzer-winning *The Late George Apley* and other mainstream novels while also turning out Mr. Moto mysteries, which would be impossible in today's more severely—and absurdly— divided worlds of popular and serious fiction. Robert Heinlein. Evan Hunter, Ed McBain, Somerset

Maugham, Keith Laumer, and so many many others.

Rex Stout.

You wondered if I was ever going to get to him, didn't you? One of the best tricks in a writer's bag is anticipation. If you set up an expectation in the reader, then draw out the fulfillment of that expectation with skill (though never at *too* great a length), he can be made to enjoy the wait and, because of waiting, can be teased to a greater appreciation of the Big Dramatic Moment than he would have if you had given it to him quickly. This technique I learned from reading Rex Stout.

I think the first Rex Stout novel I read was *The Father Hunt*, which was published in 1968, when the author was eighty-two years old. It was a Nero Wolfe story, of course, and I was swept away, drawn into the palpable atmosphere of that brownstone house on West 35th Street in Manhattan, where the fat detective and his good right hand, Archie Goodwin, lived and worked. I recall finishing the book with purest delight at what I had discovered (after resisting my wife's importunings to read one of them for, oh, two or three years), and with dismay that the author was of such an advanced age that he would never be able to write enough in this wonderful series to satisfy my new hunger for it. Then I discovered there were at that time forty-three Nero Wolfe titles, counting collections of novelettes.

Consider that Rex Stout was born in 1886, and did not write his first Nero Wolfe mystery, *Fer-de-Lance*, until 1934, when he was forty-eight years old, then proceeded to become one of the most widely published and famous mystery writers in the world. Talk about a successful second career! Or maybe it was his twenty-first career, since he sometimes claimed to have held twenty jobs between the time he finished his service in the Navy until he created the fattest and most eccentric and most brilliant detective of all time. More likely mystery writing was his first *genuine* career, as it cannot have been possible to conduct twenty others between his early twenties and late forties; everything prior to Wolfe was preparation.

By the time I read five of Stout's mysteries, I realized I was in the hands of a writer who knew a great deal about a wide variety of subjects and was mining extensive real-world experience, but I also knew that he was, like me, an omnivorous reader. His best books glow because of it. They are filled with literary allusions of exquisite subtlety, clever references and associations to the work of myriad other authors, the use of genre traditions in ways that can only be conceived by a writer who knows not merely the genre in which he works but its relationship to all other categories of fiction and to mainstream literature. Understand, he never bores you with his erudition. He never shoves it in your face. It's possible to read his books, never cotton to a single allusion, and still enjoy the hell out of them. But the reason you *can* enjoy the hell out of them is because the surface story has all those hidden supports.

I also learned from Rex Stout, among others, that popular fiction, regardless of genre, can be ambitious and can have more than a little something worthwhile to say to the reader. Archie Goodwin (who is, actually, more the central figure of this series than Nero Wolfe himself) is Huck Finn brought into the modern age,

Huck with his emancipator's soul intact but less naive, more cynical—yet strangely more hopeful, too. Nero Wolfe's exceptional intellect has allowed him to see too deeply into our modern world, and he has turned away from it, perhaps out of despair or disgust or both, taking refuge in a life of special private pleasures of the mind and body, redeemed only by a strict personal code and an adherence to the values that built civilization but which "civilized" society seems to have forgotten or abandoned. Without Archie Goodwin— the archetypal good man who wins; what a name!— Wolfe would be ineffective, a hermit and curmudgeon not worth reading about. Together, each bringing his strengths and weaknesses to the drama, they play out allegories of various aspects of the human condition with a grace that should make this series of novels timeless.

Having said all of this, I would be remiss if I did not warn the new reader that, while always engaging, these are not tales of fast action. They contain little blood—a smear there, a drop here. More often than not, the major events take place offstage, and the lead characters only discuss them after the fact! The pleasure for the reader lies, instead, in the fascination of the characters (which grows with every book one reads) and the play of the mind. The play of the mind . . . Yet these are not puzzle stories in the classic sense, like some Agatha Christie. In fact you often don't care that much *who* killed whom. Stout was concerned more with the why of murder and with exploring how essentially ethical men, like Wolfe and Goodwin, differ from the muck of humanity in their methods of thinking.

I will not claim that Stout's prose is without fault.

For the most part it is supple, so clear that it appears simpler than it really is, and strong. But in some of the books, including *Where There's A Will*, the great man trips up and shows us he's human. For example, Wolfe "snaps" his dialogue when such a manner of speaking is patently impossible; try snapping a line yourself, with the attempt to sound like thumb clicking forefinger or like a mousetrap being sprung, and you'll see what I mean; only someone wearing bad dentures has a chance of "snapping" out words, much to his embarrassment. But the slips are few and minor, and the story usually sweeps the reader along so well that the flaws are never noticed.

Rex Stout's Nero Wolfe novels had such an impact on me, in my formative years as a writer, that I now collect the hard-to-get first-edition hardcovers. They are not cheap, these rare volumes. But I've had a little writing success of my own, and I would rather indulge a sentimental streak than spend the money on cashmere socks and ancient bottles of bordeaux. If you read my books, you'll be hard-pressed to see where I write at all like Rex Stout. But a piece of him is in there; believe me.

For better or worse, this is one way a writer lives after his death, other than in his own books: in the indelible imprint he leaves when you crack the covers of his novels and give him the chance to leave his fingerprints all over your soul. It's not an invasion of privacy, but a small crime of kindness, a breaking and entering with the intention of giving rather than taking.

Enjoy.

—**Dean R. Koontz**

Where There's A Will

Chapter 1

I put the 1938–39 edition of *Who's Who in America*, open, on the leaf of my desk, because it was getting too heavy to hold on a hot day.

"They were sprinkled at discreet intervals," I stated aloud. "If they didn't fudge when they supplied the dope, April is thirty-six, May forty-one, and June forty-six. Five years apart. Apparently their parents started at the middle of the calendar and worked backwards, and also apparently they named June that because she was born in June, 1893. But the next one shows an effort of the imagination. I prefer to suppose it was Mamma who thought of it. Although the baby was actually born in February, they named it May . . ."

There was no sign that Nero Wolfe was listening as he leaned back in his chair with his eyes closed, but I went on anyhow. On that hot July day, in spite of the swell lunch Fritz had served us, I would have sold the world for a dime. My vacation was over. The news from Europe was enough to make you want to put signs at every ten yards along the seacoast, "Private

Shore. No Sharks or Statesmen Allowed." I had
bandages on my arms where the black flies had bored
for blood in Canada. Worst of all, Nero Wolfe had gone
in for a series of fantastic expenditures, the bank
balance was the lowest it had been for years, and the
detective business was rotten; and just to be contrary,
instead of doing his share of the worrying about it he
seemed to have adopted the attitude that it would be
impertinent to attempt to interfere with natural laws.
Which had me boiling. He might be eccentric enough
to find pleasure in a personal and intimate test of the
operations of the New Deal WPA, but if I had my way
about it the only meaning WPA would ever have for
yours truly would be Wolfe Pays Archie.

So I went on buzzing. "It all depends," I declared,
"on what it is that's biting them. It must be something
pretty painful, or they wouldn't have made an appointment to call on you in a body. The death of their
brother Noel has probably taken care of their financial
potentialities. Noel's in here too." I frowned at the
Who's Who. "He was forty-nine, the eldest, three
years older than June, and was next to Cullen himself
in Daniel Cullen and Company. Did it all himself,
started there as a runner in 1908 at twelve bucks a
week. That was in his obit in the *Times*, day before
yesterday. Did you read it?"

Wolfe was motionless. I made a face at him and
resumed.

"They're not due for twenty minutes yet, so I
might as well give you the benefit of my research.
There's more in this magazine article I dug up than in
Who's Who. A lot of rich and colorful details. For
instance, it says that May has worn cotton stockings

ever since the Japs bombed Shanghai. It says that
Mamma was an amazing woman because she was the
mother of four extraordinary children. I have never
understood why, in cases like this, it is assumed that
Papa's contribution was negligible, but there's no time
to go into that now. It's the extraordinary children
we're dealing with."

I flipped a page of the magazine. "To sum up about
Noel, who died Tuesday. It seems he had a row of
buttons installed on his desk in the Wall Street offices
of Daniel Cullen and Company; one for each country in
Europe and Asia, not to mention South America.
When he pressed a button, that country's government
resigned and they telephoned him to ask who to put in
next. You can't say that wasn't extraordinary. The
eldest daughter, June, was, as I say, born in June,
1893. At the age of twenty she wrote a daring and
sensational book called *Riding Bareback*, and a year
later another one entitled *Affairs of a Titmouse*. Then
she married a brilliant young New York lawyer named
John Charles Dunn, who is at the present moment the
Secretary of State of the United States of America.
He sent a cogent letter to Japan last week. The
magazine states that Dunn's meteoric rise is in great
part due to his remarkable wife. Mamma again. June
is in fact a mamma, having a son, Andrew, twenty-
four and a daughter, Sara, twenty-two."

I shifted to elevate my feet. "The other two
extraordinaries are still named Hawthorne. May
Hawthorne never has married. They are thinking of
prosecuting her under the anti-trust law for her
monopoly on brain cells. At the age of twenty-six she
revolutionized colloid chemistry, something about

bubbles and drops. Since 1933 she has been president
of Varney College, and in those six years has in-
creased its endowment funds by over twelve million
bucks, showing that she has gone from colloidal to
colossal. It says her intellectual power is extraordinary.

"I was wrong when I said the other two are still
named Hawthorne. In April's case I should have said
'again' instead of 'still'. While she was taking London
by storm in 1927 she glanced over the prostrate
nobility at her feet and picked out the Duke of Lozano.
Four other dukes, a bunch of earls and barons, and
two soap manufacturers committed suicide. But alas.
Three years later she divorced Lozano, while she was
taking Paris by storm, and became April Hawthorne
again, privately as well as publicly. She is the only
actress, alive or dead, who has played both Juliet and
Nora. At present she is taking New York by storm for
the eighth time. I can confirm that personally, because
a month ago I paid a speculator five dollars and fifty
cents for a ticket to *Scrambled Eggs*. You may remember that I tried to persuade you to go. I figured that
since April Hawthorne is the acknowledged queen of
the American stage, you owed it to yourself to see
her."

Not a flicker. He wouldn't rouse.

"Of course," I said sarcastically, "it is deplorable
that these extraordinary Hawthorne gals have no
more consideration for your privacy than to come
charging in here before you finish digesting your
lunch. No matter what is biting them, no matter if
their brother Noel left them a million dollars apiece
and they want to pay you half of it for putting a tail on

their banker, they ought to have more regard for common courtesy. When June phoned this morning I told her—"

"Archie!" His eyes opened. "I am aware that you call Mrs. Dunn, whom you have never met, by her first name, because you think it irritates me. It does. Don't do it. Shut up."

"—I told Mrs. Dunn it was an intolerable invasion of your inalienable right to sit here in peace and watch the bank balance disappear in the darkening twilight of the slow but inevitable dispersion of your mental powers and the pitiful collapse of your instinct of self-preservation—"

"Archie!" He thumped the desk.

It was time to side-step, but I was rescued from that necessity by the door's opening and the appearance of Fritz Brenner. Fritz was beaming, and I could guess why. The visitors he had come to announce had probably impressed him as something unusually promising in the way of clients. The only secrets in Nero Wolfe's old house on 35th Street near the Hudson River were professional secrets. It was unavoidable that I, his secretary, bodyguard, and chief assistant, should be aware that the exchequer was having its bottom scraped; but Fritz Brenner, cook and gentleman of the household, and Theodore Horstmann, custodian of the famous and expensive collection of orchids which Wolfe maintained in the plant rooms on the roof—they knew it too. And Fritz was beaming, obviously, because the trio whose arrival he was announcing looked more like a major fee than anything the office had seen for weeks. He did it in style. Wolfe

told him, with no enthusiasm, to show them in. I took
my feet off the desk.

Though the extraordinary Hawthorne gals did not
strongly resemble one another, my discreet glances of
appraisal as I got them arranged into chairs made it
credible that they were daughters of the same amazing mother. April I had seen on the stage; now that I
got a look at her off it, I was ready to concede that she
could probably take Nero Wolfe's office by storm if she
cared to let loose. She looked hot, peevish, beautiful
and overwhelming. When she thanked me for her
chair I decided to marry her as soon as I could save up
enough to buy a new pair of shoes.

May, the intellectual giant and college president,
surprised me. She looked sweet. Later, seeing how
determined her mouth could get, and how cutting her
voice, when the occasion required it, I made drastic
revisions, but then she just looked sweet, harmless,
and not quite middle-aged. June, Mrs. Dunn to you,
was slenderer than either of her younger sisters, next
door to skinny, with hair that was turning gray, and
restless dark burning eyes—the kind of eyes that have
never been satisfied and never will be. Where they all
looked alike was chiefly the forehead—broad, rather
high, with well-marked temple depressions and strong
eye ridges.

June did the introducing; first herself and her
sisters, and then the two males who accompanied
them. Their names were Stauffer and Prescott.
Stauffer was probably under forty, maybe five years
older than me, not a bad-looking guy if he had been a

little more careless with his face. He was living up to
something. The other one, Prescott, was nearer fifty.
He was medium-short, with a central circumference
that made it seem likely he would grunt if he bent over
to tie his shoestring. Nothing, of course, like Nero
Wolfe's globular grandeur. I recognized him from a
picture I had seen in the rotogravure when he had
been elected to something in the Bar Association. He
was Glenn Prescott of the law firm of Dunwoodie,
Prescott & Davis. He had on a Metzger shirt and tie,
and a suit that cost a hundred and fifty bucks, and
wore a flower in his buttonhole.

The flower was the cause of a little diversion right
at the beginning. I have given up trying to decide
whether Wolfe does those things just to establish the
point that he's eccentric, or because he's curious, or to
spar for time to size someone up, or what. Anyhow,
they had barely got settled in their chairs when he
aimed his eyes at Prescott and asked politely:

"Is that a centaurea?"

"I beg your pardon?" Prescott looked blank. "Oh,
you mean my buttonhole. I don't know. I just stop at
the florist's and select something."

"You wear a flower without knowing its name?"

"Certainly. Why not?"

Wolfe shrugged. "I never saw a centaurea of that
color before."

"It isn't," Mrs. Dunn put in impatiently. "A centaurea cyanus has a much closer formation—"

"I didn't say centaurea cyanus, madam." Wolfe
sounded testy. "I had in mind centaurea leucophylla."

"Oh. I've never seen one. Anyway, that isn't a
centaurea leuco-anything. It's a dianthus superbus."

April started to laugh. May smiled at her as
Einstein would smile at a kitten. June darted her eyes
that way and April stopped laughing and said in her
famous rippling voice:

"You win, Juno. It's a dianthus superbus. I don't
mind your always being right, not a bit, but when
anything strikes me as funny it's my nature to laugh.
And, I might inquire, was I dragged down here to
hear you treat the audience to a spot of botany?"

"You weren't dragged," the elderly sister retorted.
"At least not by me."

May fluttered a deprecating hand. "You must
forgive us, Mr. Wolfe. Our nerves are quite ragged.
We do wish to consult you about something serious."
She looked at me and smiled so sweetly that I smiled
back. Then she added to Wolfe, "And something
extremely confidential."

"That's all right," Wolfe assured her. "Mr. Goodwin
is my âme damnée. I could do nothing without him.
The spot of botany was my fault; I started it. Tell me
about the something serious."

Prescott inquired reluctantly, "Shall I explain?"

April, waving a hand to extinguish the match with
which she had lit a cigarette, and squinting to keep the
smoke from her eyes, shook her head at him. "Fat
chance of a man explaining anything with all three of
us present."

"I think," May suggested, "it would be better if
June—"

Mrs. Dunn said abruptly, "It's my brother's will."

Wolfe frowned at her. He hated fights about wills,
having once gone so far as to tell a prospective client
that he refused to engage in a tug of war with a dead

man's guts for a rope. But he asked not too rudely, "Is there something wrong with the will?"

"There is." June's tone was incisive. "But first I'd like to say—you're a detective. It's not a detective we need. It was my idea we should come to you. Not so much on account of your reputation, more because of what you did once for a friend of mine, Mrs. Llewellyn Frost. She was then Glenna McNair. Also I have heard my husband speak highly of you. I gathered that you had done something difficult for the State Department."

"Thank you. But," Wolfe objected, "you say you don't need a detective."

"We don't. But we very much need the services of an able, astute, discreet and unscrupulous man."

"That's diplomacy for you," said April, tapping ash from her cigarette.

It was ignored. Wolfe inquired, "What kind of services?"

I decided what it was about June's face that needed adjustment. Her eyes were the eyes of a hawk, but her nose, which should have been a beak to go with the eyes, was just a straight, good-looking nose. I preferred to look at April. But June was talking:

"Very exceptional services, I'm afraid. My husband says nothing but a miracle will do, but he's a cautious and conservative man. You know of course that my brother died on Tuesday, three days ago. The funeral was held yesterday afternoon. Mr. Prescott— my brother's attorney—collected us last evening to read the will to us. Its contents shocked and astonished us—all of us, without exception."

Wolfe made a little sound of distaste. I knew it for

that, but I suppose it might have passed for sympathy to people who had just met him. But he said dryly:

"Those disagreeable shocks would never occur if the inheritance tax were one hundred per cent."

"I suppose so. You sound like a Bolshevik. But it wasn't the disappointment of expectant legatees, it was something much worse—"

"Excuse me," May put in quietly. "In my case it was. He had told me he was leaving a million dollars to the science fund."

"I am merely saying," June declared impatiently, "that we are not hyenas. Certainly none of us was calculating on any imminent inheritance from Noel. We knew of course that he was wealthy, but he was only forty-nine and in extremely good health." She turned to Prescott. "I think, Glenn, the quickest way will be for you to tell Mr. Wolfe briefly the provisions of the will."

The lawyer cleared his throat. "I must remind you again, June, that once it is made public—"

"Mr. Wolfe will take it in confidence. Won't you?"

Wolfe nodded. "Certainly."

"Well." Prescott cleared his throat again. He looked at Wolfe. "Mr. Hawthorne left a number of small bequests to servants and employees, a total of one hundred and sixty-four thousand dollars. A hundred thousand to each of the two children of his sister, Mrs. John Charles Dunn, and a like amount to the science fund of Varney College. Five hundred thousand to his wife; he had no children. An apple to his sister June, a pear to his sister May, and a peach to his sister April." The lawyer looked uncomfortable. "I assure you that Mr. Hawthorne, who was not only my client but my friend, was not a freak. There was a statement that his sisters needed nothing of this, that he made those bequests only as symbols of his regard."

"Indeed. Does that cover the estate? Around a million?"

"No." Prescott looked even more uncomfortable. "The residue will be roughly seven million, after the deduction of taxes. Probably a little less. It was left to a woman whose name is Naomi Karn."

"La femme," said April. It was neither a sneer nor a flippancy, merely a statement of fact.

Wolfe sighed.

Prescott said, "The will was drawn by me after instructions from Mr. Hawthorne. It is dated March 7, 1938, and replaced one which had been drawn three years previously. It was kept in a vault in the office of my firm. I mention this on account of intimations made last evening by Mrs. Dunn and Miss May Hawthorne that I should have notified them of its contents at the time it was drawn. As you know, Mr. Wolfe, that would have been—"

"Nonsense," May said cuttingly. "You know very well we were upset. We were gasping."

"We still are." June's eyes pierced Wolfe. "You will please understand that my sisters and I are perfectly satisfied with our fruit. It isn't that. But think of it, the sensation and scandal of it! I can hardly believe it! None of us can. It's incredible. My brother leaving his entire fortune, the bulk of it, to that—that—"

"Woman," April suggested.

"Very well. Woman."

"It was his fortune," Wolfe observed. "And apparently that's what he did with it."

"Meaning?" May inquired.

"Meaning that if it's the sensation and scandal you object to, the less you say and do about it the sooner it will be forgotten."

"Thank you," said June sarcastically. "We need something better than that. The publication of the will alone would be bad enough. Considering that millions are involved, and the position of my husband, and of my sisters—My Lord! Don't you realize that we're the famous Hawthorne girls, whether we like it or not?"

"Of course we like it," April asserted. "We love it."

"Speak for yourself, Ape." June kept her eyes on Wolfe. "You can imagine what the papers will do. Even so, I think your advice is good. I think the best plan would be to do and say nothing, let it run its course and ignore it. But it isn't going to be allowed to run its course. Something utterly horrible is going to happen. Daisy is going to contest the will."

Wolfe's frown deepened. "Daisy?"

"Oh, excuse me. As my sister said, our nerves are in shreds. Our brother's death was a staggering shock. Then its aftermath—yesterday the funeral—and then this. Daisy is my brother's wife. His widow. She is well established as a tragic figure."

Wolfe nodded. "The lady who wears a veil."

"So you know the legend."

"Not a legend," May declared. "Much more than a legend. A fact."

"I merely share the public knowledge," said Wolfe. "Of the story that—some six years ago, I believe— Noel Hawthorne was doing archery and an arrow, which he let fly inadvertently, tore a path through his wife's face, from her brow to her chin. She had been beautiful. Since then she has never been seen without a veil."

April said, with a little shudder, "It was dreadful. I saw her in the hospital, and I still dream about it. She was the most beautiful woman I ever saw except a girl selling cigarettes in a café in Warsaw."

"She was emotionally barren," May asserted. "Like me, but without alternatives. She should never have married our brother or anyone else."

June shook her head. "You're both wrong. Daisy was too cold to be truly beautiful. The seeds of emotion were in her, waiting to germinate. The Lord knows they're bearing fruit now. We all heard the vindictiveness in her voice last night, and that's an emotion, isn't it?" June's eyes were at Wolfe again. "She implacable. She's going to make it as ugly as she can. The income from half a million dollars would be ample for her, but she's going to fight. You know what that will be like. Utterly horrible. So your advice to let the scandal run its course is inadequate. She hates the Hawthornes. My husband would be called as a witness. All of us would."

May put in, with all the sweetness gone both from her tone and her eyes, "We are going to prevent it."

"We want," said April, letting fire with her ripple, "we want you to prevent it, Mr. Wolfe."

"My husband spoke very highly of you," June stated, as if that settled everything, including the weather.

"Thank you." Wolfe sent a glance around at them,

from one to the other, including the two men. "What am I supposed to do, obliterate Mrs. Hawthorne?"

"No." June spoke with finality. "You can't do anything with her. You'll have to attack it from the other end. The woman, Naomi Karn. Get her to give up most of it—at least half of it. If you do that, we'll do the rest. For some unknown reason Daisy really wants the money, though the Lord knows what she thinks she's going to do with it. You may find it difficult, but surely not impossible. You can tell Miss Karn that if she doesn't relinquish at least half of it she'll have a fight on her hands, and she may lose considerably more than half."

"Anyone can tell her that, madam." Wolfe turned to the lawyer. "How does it stand legally? Would Mrs. Hawthorne have a case?"

"Well." Prescott screwed up his lips. "She would have a case, of course. To begin with, under the common law—"

"No, please. Don't brief it. In a word, could Mrs. Hawthorne break the will?"

"I don't know. I think she might. In view of the way the will is worded, the law leaves it open to the facts." Prescott was looking uncomfortable again. "You might appreciate that I am in an anomalous position. Dangerously close to an unethical position. I myself drew the will for Mr. Hawthorne, having been instructed by him to make it as contest-proof as possible. I cannot be expected to suggest ways and means of attack on my own document; rather it is my duty to defend it. On the other hand, as a friend of all the members of the Hawthorne family—not as an attorney—and I may say, also of Mr. Dunn, who holds a position of national eminence—I realize the incalculable harm that would result from a public trial of the issue. It is extremely desirable to avoid it if possible, and in view of the attitude Mrs. Hawthorne had unfortunately adopted—"

Prescott stopped, and screwed up his lips again. He went on, "I'll tell you. Frankly and confidentially—and it is highly unethical for me to say this—I regard that will as an outrage. I told Noel Hawthorne so at the time it was drawn, but when he insisted, all I could do was obey his instructions. Entirely aside from its unfairness to Mrs. Hawthorne, I was aware that he had told his sister he would leave a million dollars to the Varney College Science Fund, and that he was making it only ten per cent of that amount. That was worse than unfair, it came close to improbity, and I told him so. Without effect. My opinion was, and still is, that under the influence of Miss Karn he had lost his balance."

"I still don't believe it." It was May again, and she was continuing to do without sweetness. "I still believe that if Noel had decided not to do what he had said he would do, he would have told me so."

"My dear Miss Hawthorne." Prescott turned to her with his lips compressed in exasperation. "Last evening I was willing to overlook your remarks because I knew you were under the stress of a great and unexpected disappointment." There was a tremble of indignation in his voice. "But that you should dare to insinuate, here in the presence of others, that the terms of Noel's will are not in accordance with his precise instructions—my God, the man could read, couldn't he—"

"Nonsense," May interrupted cuttingly. "I was merely expressing incredulity. I would as soon attack the laws of thermodynamics as your integrity. Maybe you were both hypnotized." Suddenly and flashingly she smiled at him, and swore plaintively. "Damn it. All of this is intolerably painful. I would be for letting it go, without a word, if it weren't that Daisy's ghoulish stubbornness makes it imperative to do something. As it is, I insist that in the settlement with Miss Karn there shall be an arrangement to increase the legacy to the science fund to the figure my brother intended at the time he discussed it with me."

"Ah," Wolfe murmured. Prescott, his lips still in a tight line, nodded at him as if to say, "Just so. Ah."

June snapped at her sister. "You're only making it more difficult, May, and perhaps impossible. Anyhow, you're bluffing. I know you. You wouldn't dream of stirring up this nasty mess. If Mr. Wolfe can talk that woman into it, all right; I'm perfectly willing your fund should get the million, but the main point is Daisy and you know it. We agreed on that—"

She stopped because the door from the hall opened. Fritz, entering, approached Wolfe's desk and extended his hand with a card tray. Wolfe took the card, glanced at it, and placed it neatly under the paperweight. Then he looked at Mrs. Dunn and addressed her:

"This card says *Mrs. Noel Hawthorne.*"

They all stared.

"Oh, my God!" April blurted. May said quietly, "We should have tied her up." June arose from her chair and demanded, "Where is she? I'll see her."

"Please." Wolfe pushed air down with his palm. "She is calling on me. I'll see her myself—"

"But this is ridiculous." June stayed on her feet. "She gave us until Monday. She promised to do nothing till then. I left my son and daughter with her to make sure—"

"You left them with her where?"

"At my brother's home. Her home. We all spent the night there—not her home either, that's one reason she's acting the way she is, as a part of the residuary estate it will go to that woman and not to her—but she promised to do nothing—"

"Please sit down, Mrs. Dunn. I'd have to see her anyway, before I could accept this job. Bring Mrs. Hawthorne in, Fritz."

"There are two ladies and a gentleman with her, sir."

"Bring them all in."

Chapter 2

Four people, not counting Fritz, acting as usher, entered the office. Fritz had to bring a couple of chairs from the front room.

I like to look at faces. In a good many cases, I admit, a glance will do me, but usually they have points, of one kind or another, that will stand more of an eye. Andrew Dunn looked like a nice husky kid, with a strong resemblance to pictures I had seen of his father. His sister Sara had her mother's dark eyes of a fighting bird and the Hawthorne forehead, but her mouth and chin was something new. The other girl was a blonde in the bud who would have convinced any impartial jury that all of this great country's anatomical scenery had not been monopolized by Hollywood. Later information disclosed that her name was Celia Fleet and that she was April Hawthorne's secretary.

But though I like to look at faces, and those three were worthy of attention, the one that drew my gaze was the one I couldn't see. The story had it that Noel Hawthorne's arrow which had accidentally struck his beautiful wife had plowed diagonally across from the

brow to the chin, and what was left was there behind
that veil—with, it was said, one eye working—and
that was what I looked at. You couldn't help it. The
gray veil was fastened to her hat and extended below
her chin, and was harnessed with a strip of ribbon. No
skin was in sight except her ears. She was medium-
sized, with what would ordinarily be called a nice
youthful figure, only with the veil and knowing why it
was there, you didn't have the feeling of anything
being nice. I sat and stared at it, trying to ignore an
inclination to offer somebody a ten-spot to pull the veil
up, knowing that if it was done I'd probably offer
another ten-spot to get it pulled down again.

She didn't take the chair I placed for her. She stood
there stiff. I had the feeling she couldn't see, but she
obviously could. After the greetings, and when I was
back in my chair again, I noticed that April's fingers
were unsteady as she fumbled for a cigarette. May
was looking sweet again, but she was tense. So was
June's voice:

"My dear Daisy, this was unnecessary! We were
completely candid with you! We told you we were
going to consult Mr. Nero Wolfe. You gave us till
Monday. There was no reason whatever why you
should have any suspicion—Sara, you little devil,
what on earth are you doing? Put that away!"

"In a second, Mom." Sara's tone was urgent. "Everybody sit tight."

A dazzling flash blinded us. There were ejacula-
tions, the loudest and least gentle from Prescott. I,
having bounded up from my chair, stood feeling foolish.

Sara said composedly, "I wanted one of Nero Wolfe

sitting at his desk. Excuse it please. Hand me that
dingus, Andy."

"Go chase a snail. You darned little fool."

"Sara! Sit down!" ·

"Okay, Mom. That's all."

We stopped blinking. I was back in my chair. Wolfe
inquired dryly, "Is your daughter a professional pho-
tographer, Mrs. Dunn?"

"No. She's a professional fiend. It's this damnable
saga of the illustrious Hawthorne girls. She wants to
carry it on. She thinks she can—"

"That isn't so! I only wanted a shot—"

"Please!" Wolfe scowled across. Sara grinned at
him. He slanted his gaze upward at the veil. "Won't
you sit down, Mrs. Hawthorne?"

"I think not, thank you." Her voice gave me the
creeps and made me want to pull the veil off myself. It
was pitched high, with a strain in it that gave me the
impression it wasn't coming from a mouth. She turned
the veil on June:

"So you think my coming was unnecessary? That's
very funny. Didn't you leave Andrew and Sara and
April's secretary to guard me so I wouldn't interfere
with you?"

"No," June declared, "we didn't. For God's sake,
Daisy, be reasonable. We only wanted—"

"I have no desire to be reasonable. I'm not an
imbecile, June. It was my face Noel ruined, not my
mind." She whirled, suddenly, and unexpectedly, to
the younger sister. "By the way, April, speaking of
faces, your secretary is much better-looking than you
are. Of course she's only half your age. How brave of
you."

April kept her eyes down and said nothing.

"You can never bear to look at me, can you?" From behind the veil came a terrible little laugh, and then it turned again to June. "I didn't come here to interfere. I came because I'm suspicious and I have cause to be. You are Hawthornes—the notorious Hawthornes. Your brother was a Hawthorne. He assured me many times that I would be generously cared for. His word, generous. I knew he had that woman, he told me so—he was candid too, like you. He gave me, monthly, more money than I needed, more than I could use, to deceive me, to stop my suspicions. And now even my house is not mine!"

"My Lord, don't I know it?" June raised a hand and let it fall. "My dear Daisy, don't I know it? Can't you believe that our one desire, our one purpose—"

"No, I can't. I don't believe a word a Hawthorne says." The breath of the bitter words was fluttering the veil, but the silk harness held it in place. "Nor you, Glen Prescott. I don't trust you. Not one of you. I didn't even believe you were coming to see this Nero Wolfe, but I find you did."

She turned to confront Wolfe. "I know about you. I know a man you did something for—I used to know him. I telephoned him today to ask about you. He said you may be relied upon completely in trust, but that as an opponent you are ruthless and dangerous. He said if I asked you point-blank whether you are on my side or not, you wouldn't lie. I came here to ask you."

"Sit down, Mrs. Hawthorne."

"No. I only came to ask you that."

"Then I'll answer it." Wolfe was brusque. "I'm not on anybody's side. Not yet. I have a violent distaste for quarrels over a dead man's property. However, I am at the moment badly in need of money. I need a job. If I accept this one, I undertake to persuade Miss Naomi Karn to relinquish a large share, as large a share as possible, of Mr. Noel Hawthorne's legacy to her, in your favor. That's what these people have asked me to do. Do you want that done?"

"Yes. But as my right, not as largess from her. I would prefer to compel—"

"You would prefer to fight for it. But there's the possibility you would lose, and besides, if persuasion doesn't get satisfactory results, you can still fight. You came to see me because you don't trust these people. Is that right?"

"Yes. My husband was their brother. Glenn Prescott was his lawyer and friend. They have tried to cheat and defraud me."

"And you suspect that they came to get my assistance in further chicanery?"

"Yes."

"Well, let's dispose of that. I wish you'd sit down." Wolfe turned to me. "Archie, take this down and type it. One carbon. 'I hereby affirm that in any negotiations I may undertake regarding the will of Noel Hawthorne, deceased, I shall consider Mrs. Noel Hawthorne as one of my clients and shall in good faith safeguard her interests, and shall notify her in advance of any change in my commitments, semicolon, it being understood that a bill for her share of my fee shall be paid by her. A line for a witness.'"

I swiveled and got the machine up and rattled it off, and handed the original to Wolfe. He read it and signed it and handed it back, and I signed as witness.

Then I folded it and put it in an envelope and offered
it to Daisy Hawthorne. The hand that took it was
dead-white, with veins showing on the back, and long
thin fingers.

Wolfe asked her politely, "Will that do, madam?"

She didn't answer. She took the sheet from the
envelope, unfolded it, and read it with her head turned
to one side, using, apparently, the left eye only from
behind the veil. Then she stuffed it in her bag, turned,
and started for the door. I got up and went to open it,
but young Dunn was ahead of me, and anyway we were
both premature. She altered her course abruptly, and
was confronting April Hawthorne, close enough to touch
her; but when she lifted her hand it was to take hold of
the bottom edge of the veil.

"Look, April!" she demanded. "I wouldn't care to
have the others see—but just for you—as a favor, you
know, in memory of Leo—"

"Don't!" April screamed. "Don't let her!"

There was commotion. Most of them were out of
their chairs. The one who got there first was Celia
Fleet, living up to her name. I didn't know a blonde's
eyes could blaze the way hers did as she faced the veil.
"You do that again," she said furiously, "and I'll pull
that thing off of you! I swear I will! Try it!"

A masculine voice horned in. "Get away from here!
Get out!" It was Mr. Stauffer, the chap who kept his
face arranged. It was now fierce with indignation, as
he shouldered Celia Fleet aside to stand protectively
in front of April, who had shrunk back in her seat and
covered her face with her hands. The same terrible
little laugh came from behind the veil, then Noel
Hawthorne's widow turned and started again for the

door. But again, halfway there, she halted to speak, this time to Mrs. Dunn.

"Don't send the brats to guard me, June. I'll keep my word. I'll give you till Monday."

Then she went. Fritz was there in the hall, looking concerned on account of the scream he had heard, and I was glad to leave it to him to escort her out the front door. That damn veil got on my nerves. As I rejoined the scene, April's shoulders were having spasms and Mr. Stauffer was patting one of them and Celia Fleet the other. May and June were quietly observing the operation. Prescott was mopping his face with his handkerchief. I asked if I should get some brandy or something.

"No, thank you." May smiled at me. "My sister is always teetering on the edge of things, more or less. I doubt if she could be a good actress if she weren't. It seems that artists have to. It used to be attributed to the flames of genius, but now they say it's glands."

April's face, pale with revulsion, came into view and she blurted, "Stop it!"

"Yes," June put in, "I don't think that's necessary, May." She looked at Wolfe. "I imagine you'll agree I was correct when I said our sister-in-law is implacable."

Wolfe nodded. "I do. Badly as I need money, I wouldn't attempt to persuade her to relinquish anything. Speaking of money, I have an exaggerated opinion of the value of my services."

"I know you have. Your bill, if it is short of outrageous, will be paid."

"Good—Archie, your notebook—Now. You want a signed agreement with Miss Karn. Half of the residuary estate, more if possible, to Mrs. Hawthorne. In addition to the half million she gets?"

"I don't know—whatever you can."

"And nine hundred thousand to the Varney College Science Fund?"

"Yes," May said positively.

"If you can get it, of course," said June. "Don't let my sister give you the idea that she'll smash the settlement if that isn't in it. She's bluffing."

May said quietly, "You've been wrong about me before, June."

"Maybe I have, but not now. Let's jump that fence when we get to it, Mr. Wolfe."

"Very well. If we can get it, we will. What about you and your sister? What do you want for yourselves?"

"Nothing. We have our fruit."

"Indeed." Wolfe looked at May. "Is that correct, Miss Hawthorne?"

"Certainly. I want nothing for myself."

Wolfe looked at the youngest. "And you?"

"What?" asked April vaguely.

"I am asking, do you demand a share of your brother's estate?"

"Good heavens, no."

"Not that we couldn't use it," said June. "April lives at least a year ahead of her income and is in debt to her ears. May washes her own stockings. She never has anything because she gives half her salary to Varney girls who would have to leave college if she didn't. As for me, I have trouble paying the grocery bills. My husband had a good income from his private practice, but the salary of a secretary of state is pretty skimpy."

"Then I think we should be able to persuade Miss Karn—"

"No. Don't try it. If my brother had left us something we could certainly have used it—and I suppose we're all surprised that he didn't. But no—no haggling for it. From him direct, yes, but not by way of that woman."

"If I get it, will you take it?"

"Don't try. Don't tempt us. You know how it is. You're in need of money yourself."

"We'll see. What about your children?"

"They get a hundred thousand apiece."

"Is that satisfactory?"

"Of course. My Lord, they're rich."

"Is anything else wanted from Miss Karn for anyone at all?"

"No."

Wolfe looked at the lawyer. "What about it, Mr. Prescott? Have you any comments?"

Prescott shook his head. "None. I'm happy to stay as well out of it as I can. I drew the will."

"So you did." Wolfe frowned at him, then transferred the frown to June. "So much for that. We'll get all we can. Now what about Miss Karn?"

"What about her?"

"Who is she, what is she, where is she?"

"I don't know much about her." June turned to the lawyer. "You tell him, Glenn."

"Well . . ." Prescott rubbed his nose. "She's a young woman, a year or two short of thirty I should say—"

"Wait a minute!" The interruption came from Sara Dunn, the professional fiend, as she glided up to Wolfe's desk with something in her hand. "Here, Mr. Wolfe, look at this. I brought it along because I thought it might be needed. That's her laughing, and the man with her is Uncle Noel. You can borrow it if you want to, but I'll want it back."

"Where in the name of heaven," Mrs. Dunn demanded, "did you get that thing?"

"Oh, I took it one day last spring when I happened to see Uncle in front of Hartlespoon's, and I knew who it must be with him. They didn't see me snap it. It's a good shot, so I had it enlarged."

"You—you knew—" June was sputtering. "How did you know about that woman?"

"Don't be a goof, Mom," said Sara sympathetically. "I wasn't born deaf, and I'm past twenty-one. You were just my age when you wrote *Affairs of a Titmouse*."

"Thank you very much, Miss Dunn." Wolfe put the picture under a paperweight on top of Daisy Hawthorne's card. "I'll remember to return it." He turned to the lawyer. "About Miss Karn? You know her, do you?"

"Not very well," said Prescott. "That is—I've known her, in a way, for about six years. She was a stenographer in our office—my firm."

"Indeed. Your personal stenographer?"

"Oh, no. We have thirty or more of them—it's a large office. She was just one of them for a couple of years, and then she became the secretary of the junior partner, Mr. Davis. It was in Mr. Davis's office that Mr. Hawthorne first met her. Not long after that—"

Prescott stopped, and looked uncomfortable. "But that's of no present significance. I wished to explain how I happened to know her. She left our employ about three years ago—uh—apparently at the suggestion of Mr. Hawthorne—"

"Apparently?"

"Well—" Prescott shrugged. "Admittedly, then. Since he himself made no attempt to be secretive about it, there is no call for caution from me."

"The Hawthornes," said May sweetly, "are much too egotistic to be sneaks. 'How we apples swim.'"

"Obviously he wasn't sneaking," Wolfe agreed, glancing at the picture under the paperweight, "when he paraded with her on Fifth Avenue."

"I think I should warn you," Prescott said, "that your task will be a difficult one."

"I expect it to be. To persuade anybody to turn loose of four million dollars."

"I know, but I mean exceptionally difficult." Prescott shook his head doubtfully. "God knows I wish you luck, but from what I know of Miss Karn . . . it'll be a job. Ask Stauffer, he'll tell you what he thinks of it. That's why we asked him to come down here with us."

"Stauffer?"

A voice came from the left: "I'm Osric Stauffer."

Wolfe looked at the good-looking face that was living up to something. "Oh. Are you . . ." He trailed it off.

The face looked faintly annoyed. "Osric Stauffer of Daniel Cullen and Company. The foreign department was under the direction of Mr. Hawthorne and I was next to him. Also I was fairly intimate with him."

So it was Daniel Cullen and Company he was living

up to. Judging from the way he had been hovering in the neighborhood of April Hawthorne, I had guessed wrong entirely; I had thought he was dignifying a passion.

Wolfe inquired, "You know Miss Karn, do you?"

"I have met her, yes." Stauffer's voice was clipped and precise. "What Mr. Prescott was referring to, I went to see her this morning about this will business. I was requested to go by him and Mrs. Dunn—and in a way, unofficially, as a representative of my firm. A will contest—this sort of thing—would be highly undesirable in the case of a Cullen partner."

"So you saw Miss Karn this morning?"

"Yes."

"What happened?"

"Nothing. I made no headway at all. Naturally, in my position, I have been entrusted with some difficult and delicate negotiations, and I've dealt with some tough customers, but I've never struck anything tougher than Miss Karn. Her position was that it would be improper, and even indecent, to interfere with the wishes of a dead man as he had himself expressed them, with regard to the disposal of his own property. Therefore she couldn't even discuss it, and she wouldn't. I told her she would have a contest to fight and might lose it all. She said she had a great respect for justice and would cheerfully accept any decision a court might make, provided there was no higher court to appeal to."

"Did you offer terms?"

"No, not specific terms. I didn't get that far. She was—" Stauffer seemed momentarily embarrassed how to put it. "She wasn't inclined to listen to anything about the will, the purpose of my call. She attempted to presume on our comparatively slight acquaintance."

"Do you mean she tried to make love to you?"

"Oh, no." Stauffer blushed, glanced involuntarily at April Hawthorne, and blushed more. "No, not that, not at all. I mean merely that she acted as if my visit were—just a friendly visit. She is an extremely clever woman."

"And you think she wasn't scared by the threat of a contest?"

"I'm positive she wasn't. I never saw anyone less scared."

Wolfe grunted. He turned to June with a frown. "What's the point," he demanded, "of asking me to bring your game down with ammunition that's already been fired?"

"That *is* the point," June asserted. "That's why we came to you. If a simple threat would do it, it would have been simple. I know it's a hard job. That's why we'll gladly pay the fee you'll charge, if you succeed."

"It is also," May put in, "why something my sister said to you at the beginning was untrue. She said we didn't need a detective, but we do. You will have to find a way to bring pressure on Miss Karn much more compelling than threat of a court contest of the will."

"I see." Wolfe grimaced. "No wonder I don't like fights about dead men's property. They're always ugly fights."

"This one isn't," June declared. "It will be if Daisy and that woman get it into a court, but our part of it isn't. What's ugly about our trying to avoid a stinking scandal by persuading that woman that three or four million dollars of our brother's fortune is all she's entitled to? If her avarice and stubbornness make the persuasion difficult and expensive . . ."

"And even if it were ugly," said May quietly, "it would still have to be done. I think, Mr. Wolfe, we've told you everything you need to know. Will you do it?"

Wolfe looked at the clock on the wall. I felt sorry for him. He didn't like the job, but he had to take it. Moreover, he permitted nothing whatever to interfere with his custom of spending four hours a day in the plant rooms on the roof—from nine to eleven in the morning and from four to six in the afternoon—and the clock said five minutes to four. He looked at me, gave me a scowl for my grin, and glanced up at the clock again.

He rose from his chair as abruptly as his bulk would permit.

"I'll do it," he announced gruffly. "And now, if you don't mind, I have an appointment for four o'clock—"

"I know!" Sara Dunn exclaimed. "You're going up to the orchids. I'd love to see them—"

"Some other time, Miss Dunn. I'm in no mood for it. Shall I report to you, Mrs. Dunn? Or Mr. Prescott?"

"Either. Or both." June was out of her chair.

"Both, then. Get names and addresses, Archie."

I did so. Prescott's office and home, the Hawthorne house on 67th Street, where they all were temporarily, and, not least important, Naomi Karn's apartment on Park Avenue. They straggled into the hall, and I left the front to Fritz. Stauffer, I noticed, was solicitous at April Hawthorne's elbow. May was the last one out of the office, having lingered for a word with Wolfe which I didn't catch. I heard the front door close, and Fritz glanced in on his way back to the kitchen.

"Pfui!" said Wolfe.

"And wowie," I agreed. "But at that they're not vultures. I'm going to marry April. Then after a bit I'll divorce her and marry her blond secretary—"

"That will do. Confound it, anyway. Well, you have two hours—"

"Sure." I assumed a false cheerfulness. "Let me say it for you. I am to have Miss Karn here at six o'clock. Or a few minutes before, so as not to keep you waiting."

He nodded. "Say ten minutes to six."

It was too damned hot to throw something at him. I merely made a disrespectful noise, beat it out to the sidewalk where the roadster was parked, climbed in, and was on my way.

Chapter 3

I suppose altogether, in business and out, I've had dealings of one kind or another with more than a hundred baby dolls. I was more or less taking it for granted that my call on Naomi Karn that afternoon would add one more to the number, but I was wrong. As the maid escorted me through the large and luxurious foyer of the apartment on the twelfth floor, on Park Avenue near 74th—where I had got admitted by saying I was sent by Mr. Glenn Prescott—and ushered me into a cool dim room with cool summer covers on the furniture, and I got close enough for a good look at the woman standing by the piano bench, I saw right away that I was wrong.

She smiled. I wouldn't say she smiled at me, she just smiled. "Mr. Goodwin? Sent by Mr. Prescott?"

"That's right, Miss Karn."

"I suppose I should have refused to see you. Only I don't like to do that—it's so stuffy."

"Why should you have refused to see me?"

"Because, if you were sent by Mr. Prescott, you've come to bully me. Haven't you?"

"Bully you about what?"

"Oh, come now." She smiled again.

I waited a second, saw that she wasn't going to add to it, and said, "As a matter of fact, I wasn't sent by Prescott. I was sent by Nero Wolfe. He has been engaged by Noel Hawthorne's sisters to discuss Hawthorne's will with you."

"Nero Wolfe, the detective?"

"That's the one."

"How interesting. When is he coming to see me?"

"He never goes to see anybody. He dislikes motion. He passed a law making it a criminal offense for his feet to remove him from his house except on rare occasions, and never on business. He hires me to run around inviting people to come to see him."

Her brows lifted. "Do you mean you came to invite me?"

"That's right. There's no hurry. It's only 4:30, and he doesn't expect you until ten minutes to six."

She shook her head. "I'm sorry. It would be interesting to discuss something with Nero Wolfe."

"Then come ahead."

"No." It sounded final. In fact, it sounded as near irrevocable as any "no" I ever heard.

I looked at her. There was no indication whatever of any strain of baby doll in her that I could see. She was close to something new in my experience. She wasn't homely and she wasn't pretty. She was dark rather than light, but she wouldn't have been listed as brunette. None of her features would have classified for star billing, but somehow you didn't see her features, you just saw her. As a matter of fact, after exchanging only a couple of sentences with her, I was sore. During nine years of detective work I had polished up my brass so that I regarded a rude stare at any human face nature's fancy could devise merely as a matter of routine, but there was something in Naomi Karn's eyes, or back of them, or somewhere, that made me want to meet them and shy away from them at the same time. It wasn't the good old come-hither, the "welcome" on the door mat that biology uses for tanglefoot; I can slide through that like molasses through a tin horn. It was something as feminine as that, it was a woman letting a man have her eyes, but it was also a good deal more—like a cocky challenge from a cocky brain. I knew I had looked away from it, and I knew she knew I had, and I was sore.

"The truth is," I said, "this thing has been handled incompetently. I understand that fellow Stauffer came to see you this morning and said if you didn't divvy us, Hawthorne's widow was going to contest it."

She smiled. "Yes, Ossie tried to say something like that."

"Ossie? Good name for him."

"I think so. I'm glad you like it."

"I do. But Ossie was deceiving you. The real point of the thing is much sharper than a court contest and it's apt to hurt more."

"Dear me. That's alarming. What is it?"

I shook my head. "I'm not supposed to tell you. But this room is the coolest place I've been in today. I could give you a piece of marvelous advice if I felt like it. What are those things with four legs, chairs?"

A breath of a laugh came out of her. "Do sit down, Mr.———"

"Goodwin. Archie."

"Do sit down." She moved. It would have been a pleasure to watch her move if I hadn't been sore at her. She wasn't as graceful or overwhelming as April Hawthorne, but her motion was just as easy, and more straightforward, without any tricks. She was pushing a button. "What kind of a drink would you like?"

"I could use a glass of milk, thank you." I selected a chair two paces away from the one she was taking. The maid entered, and was instructed to bring a glass of milk and a bottle of Borrand water. Miss Karn refused the cigarette I offered. When I had mine lit she remarked:

"You have alarmed me, you know. Terribly." She sounded amused. "Will the milk make you feel like surrendering the advice?"

"I feel like it already." I met her eyes and went on meeting them. "I advise you not to see Nero Wolfe. I'm being disloyal, of course, but I'm naturally treacherous anyhow, and besides, I don't like the way they're ganging up on you. I felt that way already, even before I saw you, but now . . ." I waved a hand.

"Now treachery is sweet."

"It could be."

"That's very nice of you. Why do you advise me not to see Nero Wolfe?"

"Because I know the kind of trap he's setting. What you should do is get a lawyer, a good one, and let Wolfe deal with him."

She made a face. "I don't like lawyers. I know too much about them—I worked for a law firm for three years."

"You'll have to hire a lawyer if there's a contest."

"I suppose I will. But you said I am threatened by

something more dangerous than a contest. That trap Nero Wolfe is setting. What's that like?"

I grinned at her and shook my head. The maid came with the liquids, and after Miss Karn's Borrand water was poured and iced I took a sip of my milk. It was a little too cold, and I wrapped the glass with my palms, grinned again, and said, "It certainly is nice and cool here. I'm enjoying myself. Are you?"

"No," she said, with a sudden and surprising sharpness in her tone, "I am not enjoying myself. A good friend of mine has died—just three days ago. Mr. Noel Hawthorne. Another man whom I regarded as my friend to a certain extent—at least not an enemy—is acting abominably. Mr. Glenn Prescott. He came here last evening and informed me of the terms of the will with a manner and tone that was inexcusable. Now he is openly conspiring with Mr. Hawthorne's family against me. He sent that Stauffer here to threaten me. He sent you here with your childish babble about traps and treachery. Bah! Is your milk all right?"

"Yes. Excuse me, but like hell you're not enjoying yourself. Shall we discuss it seriously?"

"I have no desire to discuss it at all. The one sensible thing you've said was that it has been handled incompetently. To send Ossie here to threaten me! I can make him stammer by looking at him! Incidentally, I can't do that with you."

"No, but you came close to it." I grinned at her. "Also you have an idea that another twenty minutes will do the trick; that's why you invited me to sit down. You may be right, but I can assure you I'm no Ossie. The fact is, I'm just killing time. My boss asked

me to bring you to his house, down on 35th Street, at
ten to six, but I'd prefer not to get you there until ten
after. He needs a lesson about what to expect and
what not to expect." I glanced at my wrist. "We ought
to be leaving fairly soon, at that. I had to park over
east of Third Avenue."

"I told you, Mr. Goodwin, that I'm not enjoying
myself. I see you have finished your milk."

"No more, thank you. So you don't intend to
come?"

"Certainly not."

"What are you going to do, just refuse to say boo
till you're served with a summons and complaint?"

"I'm not refusing to say boo." Her voice got sharp
again. "I tell you, what I resent is the way they've
gone about it. I know that nothing rational could be
expected of Mrs. Hawthorne, but couldn't Mrs. Dunn
have come to see me, or asked me to come to see her,
and talk it over? Couldn't she have said simply that
they regarded it as unjust and asked me to consider an
adjustment? Couldn't she have condescended to say
that she and her sisters felt they had a natural right to
some share in their brother's estate?"

"But they didn't. That wasn't it. It's Daisy that's
raising hell."

"I don't believe it. I think Glenn Prescott started
it, and they helped him prevail upon Mrs. Hawthorne.
They think the way to do it is to browbeat me. First
they sent that Stauffer here, and then they hired a
detective, Nero Wolfe, whose speciality is catching
murderers. You might think I was a murderer myself.
It won't work. They may be perfectly correct in
thinking they should have a slice of Noel's—Mr.

Hawthorne's wealth, but if they get it now it will be because a court awards it to them."

"Okay," I agreed. "I'm with you. Absolutely. They're a bunch of wolverines, Prescott is a two-faced shyster, and Stauffer is Ossie. But may I ask you a hypothetical question?"

"It would take more than a hypothetical question to make me budge, Mr. Goodwin."

"I'll ask it anyway. It'll be good exercise for us and pass the time. Let's say, of course just as a hypothesis, that Nero Wolfe is ruthless, unscrupulous, and quite cunning; that you get him sore by refusing even to go and discuss it with him; that he's out to do you; that he gets the bright idea of basing the attack on the will, not on the ground that it's unfair, but on the ground that it's phony; that he is able—"

"So that's it." Miss Karn's eyes were going through me. "That's the new threat, is it? It's no better than the other one, not even as good. Didn't Mr. Prescott himself draw the will? Wasn't it in his possession?"

"Sure it was. That's the point. It's your own idea that he's conspiring against you, isn't it? Since he drew the will and had it in his possession, isn't he in an ideal position to support Wolfe's contention that there has been a substitution and the will's a phony?"

"No. He couldn't. He is on record as accepting the will's authenticity."

"On record with who? Wolfe and the Hawthornes. His fellow conspirators."

"But—" She chopped it off. Her eyes had narrowed and she sat motionless. In a moment she said slowly, "Mr. Prescott wouldn't do that. After all, he is an attorney of high standing and reputation—"

"Your opinion of him seems to be going up."

"My opinion of him is unimportant. But another thing, if he intended to play as dirty a trick as that, he could simply have not produced it. He could have destroyed it."

"He had no such intention. The hypothesis is that Wolfe gets the idea and sells it to them. Didn't I say it was hypothetical?"

"Yes. You said so." Her eyes got narrower. "Is it? Or is this what Nero Wolfe has got ready for me?"

I lifted the shoulders. "You'll have to ask him, Miss Karn. All I know is this, he wants you to come and discuss it with him. He has engaged to try to persuade you to agree to some sort of a settlement. I've never known anybody to make bingo by refusing to talk with Wolfe when he wants to talk."

She looked through me for another ten seconds, and then abruptly got up without bothering to excuse herself, and left the room. I arose too and strolled over to the archway and stood there with an ear cocked, thinking I might hear some telephoning or something, but the apartment was too big or too soundproof, and I drew a blank. Fifteen minutes passed, and I had about decided on a tour of exploration, when the sound of footsteps came, and I got back to the middle of the room by the time she entered. She had changed to a blue linen thing, with a flowing wrap of the same, and had on a kind of a hat. She announced, merely imparting information:

"I'm not going because I'm scared. Not that that matters to you. Your job was to get me there. Come on."

There was no question but that she got the gist of

things with a minimum of effort and time. Down on the sidewalk I discovered that she was nice to walk with. At that juncture of affairs she had about as much use for me as a robin has for a black snake, but since we were walking together she let it be a partnership instead of a game of tag. Most girls, walking along a busy sidewalk with you, are either clingers, divers, or laggers, and I don't know which is worst.

There was no conversation, even after we got to the roadster and climbed in and nosed it into the traffic. That suited me. The gambit I had used to pry her loose had been impromptu. It wasn't going to get me any medal from the boss, and I had to figure out a way of conveying to him its purely hypothetical nature in a diplomatic manner. Not that he would object to being portrayed as ruthless, unscrupulous and cunning, but he certainly wouldn't be enthusiastic about my giving her the impression that he was a boob. The thing to do was to deposit her in the front room and have a few words alone with him before introducing her. It would have been better to have the few words up in the plant rooms, but that was out because it was 6:15 when we arrived and he would already be back down in the office, waiting for us.

My scheme didn't pan out. Three cars parked at the curb warned me to expect competition. I opened the door with my key and ushered her into the hall, and there was Fritz Brenner approaching to head us off.

"Company?" I asked.

He nodded. "The ladies and gentlemen who were here this afternoon. They have returned. They arrived at three minutes to six."

"You don't say." I addressed Miss Karn: "This is unexpected and unfortunate. I guess you'll have to wait a few minutes." I moved toward the door to the front room. "In here it won't be as cool as up at your place—"

She was moving too, and so swiftly that I couldn't head her off. I suppose I should have been on my guard, but how could I have known she would make a beeline for the office door, spotting it by instinct, and bust on through? I bounced after her, but by the time I reached the threshold she was already inside and in the middle of them. I put on the brakes and let it come.

They were all there, the whole gang except the widow with the veil. The Hawthorne girls were merely regarding the intruder with surprise, but there was a little squeal from Sara Dunn and a pair of startled exclamations from Osric Stauffer and Glenn Prescott. The intruder, paying no attention to any of them, advanced clear to the desk, faced Wolfe, and said calmly:

"You're Nero Wolfe? I'm Naomi Karn. I'm told you want to discuss something with me."

June muttered, "Good Lord."

May craned her neck for a better look.

April laughed out loud and said energetically, "Curtain. Absolutely curtain."

Wolfe had his lips pursed. Before he got them open for words, Miss Karn whirled to Glenn Prescott:

"Is it true that you're in a plot to have that will declared a forgery? Answer me!"

The lawyer gaped at her. "What's that?" he sputtered. "A plot to—a forgery—what the devil—"

"I insist it was a curtain," April declared. Her sisters were saying something too, and Stauffer was shushing her, and Prescott and Miss Karn were making it a free-for-all, with nothing emerging for the record, until Wolfe's voice came out on top:

"That will do! Ladies and gentlemen! My office is not a barnyard!" He gave me a withering glance. "Confound you, Archie!" He switched to the lawyer. "Mr. Prescott, I beg your pardon for having in my employ a young man whose soaring imagination alights on such clichés as sinister plots and forged wills—As for you, Miss Karn, I presume you think you are being audacious and intrepid—"

"Positively Penthesilean," May inserted.

Wolfe ignored it. "Taking the bull by the horns. Pfui! It should be possible to adhere to the code of ordinary decent manners even when fighting for a fortune. It should also be possible for a young woman with eyes as intelligent as yours to avoid being hoodwinked by Mr. Goodwin's elephantine capers. It may be, I admit, that you were disconcerted because, coming here expecting a private interview with me, you found these people here. That was not my fault, nor theirs. They did not know you were coming, nor did I know they were. They came, unannounced, to tell me that Mrs. Noel Hawthorne, immediately after leaving my office this afternoon, proceeded to engage a lawyer, and that he has already made formal application to Mr. Prescott for a copy of the will. As you see, you're not the only one—Yes, Fritz?"

Fritz had entered in his grand manner, but an unexpected bump in his right rear cramped his style. My eyes widened as I saw who it was that had

accidentally bumped him, brushing past—our old
friend Inspector Cramer of the homicide squad. At his
heels was that pillar of pessimism, District Attorney
Skinner, and in the rear was a bony little runt with a
mustache, carrying last year's straw hat. Fritz,
bumped, seeing there was nothing left for him to
announce, stepped aside and tried not to glare with
indignation.

Wolfe's voice sang out, "How-do-you-do, gentlemen! As you see, I'm busy. If you will kindly—"

"That's all right, Mr. Wolfe." Skinner, his deep
bass croaking, pushed in front of Cramer. He glanced
around at the faces. "Mrs. John Charles Dunn? I'm
District Attorney Skinner. Miss May Hawthorne?
Miss April Hawthorne? I have some—uh—unpleasant
news for you." He sounded apologetic. "It was necessary to find you at once—"

"Permit me, sir," Wolfe snapped at him. "This is
intolerable! We are conferring on a private matter—"

"I'm sorry," said Skinner. "Believe me, I am sorry.
Our business is extremely urgent, or we wouldn't
come barging in like this. We wish to make some
inquiries regarding the death of Mr. Noel Hawthorne
last Tuesday afternoon. At your place in the country
up near Nyack, wasn't it, Mrs. Dunn?"

"Yes." June's dark eyes were piercing him. "What
do you—why do you wish to inquire about it?"

"Because that is our unpleasant duty." Skinner met
her gaze. "Because we are confronted by evidence that
your brother's death was not accidental. Evidence, in
fact, that he was murdered."

There was dead silence. Good and dead.

Skinner and Cramer were taking in faces, and I

took them in too. I was close enough to April so that when her lips moved I caught the whispered breath of the two syllables, "Curtain," but her pallor and her staring eyes told me that she wasn't aware she had breathed at all.

Chapter 4

Wolfe heaved a deep sigh. Prescott got to his feet, opened his mouth, shut it again, and sat down. Osric Stauffer emitted a sound suggestive of shocked and indignant disbelief, which went unnoticed.

June, her eyes still piercing Skinner, said, "That's impossible." Her voice went a little higher: "Quite impossible!"

"I wish it were, Mrs. Dunn," he declared. "I sincerely do. No one realizes better than I do what this will mean to all of you—your husband and your sisters—all the regrettable aspects of it—and it was with the greatest reluctance—almost unconquerable reluctance—"

"That's a lie." The voice came from May Hawthorne, but it was a new one. It snapped like a whip. "Let's take this as it is, Mr. Skinner. Don't snivel about reluctance. We know the smell of politics. This means it has been decided that you can use my brother's death to finish off my brother-in-law. Perhaps you can. Go ahead and try, but spare us the cant."

Skinner, looking at her and letting her finish, said with composure, "You're wrong, Miss Hawthorne. I assure you it was with deep and genuine reluctance—"

"Do you deny that for the past two months your crowd has been spreading calumny regarding my brother-in-law and his relations with my brother?"

"Yes, I do deny it. I belong to no crowd, unless you mean my political party. I have heard gossip, a good many people have—"

"Do you deny—"

"Don't, May," commanded June, taking over. "What's the use?" Her eyes darted to Skinner again. "You stated that you have evidence that my brother was murdered. What is the evidence?"

"I'll tell you that shortly, Mrs. Dunn. Before it can be known exactly what the evidence means it will be necessary to ask for a little information from you. That's why—"

"May I ask a question?" came from Glenn Prescott.

"Certainly." Skinner nodded at his professional brother. "I'm glad you're here, Prescott. Not that I propose to give Mrs. Dunn any reason to consult an attorney, but I'm glad you're here, anyway."

"So am I," said Prescott succinctly. "For one thing, if there was a murder, it was in Rockland County, wasn't it?"

"Yes." Skinner turned abruptly to indicate the bony undersized person with the straw hat still in his hand. "This is Mr. B. A. Regan, district attorney of Rockland County. Mr. Regan, of course you've heard of Glenn Prescott, of Dunwoodie, Prescott & Davis."

"Sure I have," Mr. Regan declared. "It's a pleasure."

Prescott nodded curtly. "I see."

"Mr. Regan came to consult my office. If you would prefer to have him do the talking—"

"Not at all. Go ahead. But another point—not a legal one, but still a point—you say you have evidence that Noel Hawthorne was murdered at the home of John Charles Dunn, while he was a guest there, and when Mr. Dunn was present. Wouldn't it have been usual and proper to advise Mr. Dunn himself first of all? Instead of broadcasting it? Particularly in view of his eminent position? Instead of tracing Mrs. Dunn to this place and bursting in here and blurting it in her face in the presence of a throng of people?"

The skin around the district attorney's mouth and eyes had tightened. He said, "I don't like your tone, Prescott."

"Never mind my tone. What about my questions?"

"Nor your questions either. However, I'll answer them. I tried for an hour to communicate with Mr. Dunn. As you must know, he is in Washington appearing before a Senate committee. I couldn't get to him. Meanwhile I learned that Mrs. Dunn and her sisters had come to the office of Nero Wolfe. I have not broadcast this thing. Nothing would please me better than not to have to broadcast it at all. I am a political opponent, a bitter opponent, of Secretary Dunn and the administration he adorns, but by God, I don't fight with stink bombs and you ought to know it, whether Miss May Hawthorne does or not. Your insinuation that I came after Mrs. Dunn because I shied at tackling Dunn himself is unwarranted and offensive. Mr. Regan came and laid evidence before me and asked my help. Before the evidence can be interpreted

with certainty, information is needed from Mrs. Dunn
and probably others. I request her, and others if
necessary, to co-operate with me in the performance
of my duty."

Prescott, looking utterly unimpressed, demanded,
"What's the evidence?"

"I don't know. I can't know until I get the information I want. I merely need some facts. Do you think
I'm going to try any dodges with you sitting here?"

Skinner turned to Wolfe. "If you'd like us to move
out of your office, perhaps—"

Wolfe shook his head. "Your business is more
urgent than mine, sir. Archie, Fritz, more chairs."

Fritz and I brought some from the front room.
Naomi Karn had faded into the background, over by
the bookshelves, and I gave her one there. She looked,
I thought, pasty. The three youngsters moved to
make room, Andrew Dunn closer to his mother, the
others to the rear. Inspector Cramer went to the hall
and came in again, accompanied by my old pal Sergeant Purley Stebbins, who ignored my greeting as he
grabbed a chair from me, planted himself on it at a
corner of my desk, and got out a notebook and pencil.
My toe unfortunately rubbed against his shin as I got
back to my own chair.

Prescott said to Nero Wolfe, "Your—" He thumbed
at me. "This man takes shorthand?"

"Yes. Archie, your notebook, please."

I leered at Purley and got it out in time to catch
Skinner's opening:

"All I want, Mrs. Dunn, is some facts. I earnestly
desire to make it as little painful as possible. There
was a gathering of people at your country home in

Rockland County last Tuesday, July 11th, was there not?"

"Yes." June turned to Prescott. "I want to say, Glenn, that I regard it as quite likely that May is right about this being a political ambush."

"So do I."

"Then should I answer this gentleman?"

"Yes," said Prescott grimly. "If you refuse to it will be worse. I'm here and if he—I can stop you. We'll have a record of it."

"I wish John was here. I'd like to telephone him."

"I doubt if you could get him. Trust me for this, June. And don't forget your son is here. He's a lawyer too, you know. What's your advice, Andy?"

The kid patted his mother on the shoulder and said in a husky voice meant to be reassuring, "Go ahead, Mom. If he tries to get slick—"

"I won't," said Skinner brusquely. "What was the gathering, Mrs. Dunn?"

"It was to celebrate our twenty-fifth wedding anniversary." June met his eye and spoke clearly and composedly. "That's why my brother was there. I mean by that, my husband and my brother had not been together for some time. We were all aware of the slander that was being whispered about the loan to Argentina, and they thought it best not to give it color—"

"That isn't necessary, June," Prescott put in. "If I were you I'd let backgrounds alone and stick to facts."

"Yes, please do," Skinner agreed. "Who was present?"

"My husband. I. Our son, Andrew. My daughter, Sara—no, Sara got there after—afterwards, with Mr.

Prescott. My sister May and my sister April. My
brother and his wife. Mr. Stauffer, Osric Stauffer. It
was a family party, but Mr. Stauffer came to give my
brother a business message and was invited to stay.
That's all."

"Excuse me. I was there."

June turned to the voice. "Oh, so you were, Celia.
I beg your pardon. Miss Celia Fleet, my sister April's
secretary."

"Is that all, Mrs. Dunn?"

"Yes."

"Servants?"

"Only a man and wife, country people. She cooks
and he works outdoors. It is a modest place and we
live on a modest scale."

"Their names, please?"

"I know 'em," said Mr. Regan.

"Good. Now, Mrs. Dunn, let's do it this way. You
know, of course, that Dr. Gyger, the medical examiner
of Rockland County, and Mr. Bryant, the sheriff, were
summoned there and came. They asked some questions and took notes, and I have read those notes.
About 4 o'clock in the afternoon your brother took a
shotgun and went to the fields to shoot crows. Is that
right?"

"No. He went to shoot a hawk."

"But I understand he shot two crows."

"Maybe he did, but he went to shoot a hawk. He
discussed it with my husband, and that's what he went
to do."

"Very well. He did shoot two crows. The shots
were heard at the house, weren't they?"

"Yes."

"And your brother did not return. At a quarter to six your son, Andrew, and a young woman—you, I believe, Miss Fleet—emerging from a wood—stumbled upon his body. Half his head had been blown off by the shotgun, which was lying near by. Your son remained there and Miss Fleet went to the house, the other side of the woods some four hundred yards distant, to notify Mr. Dunn. Mr. Dunn himself telephoned to New City. Sheriff Bryant, with a deputy, arrived at the scene at 6:35, and Dr. Gyger a few minutes later. They came to the conclusion that Hawthorne had tripped on a briar—the body lay in a patch of briars—or that the gun's trigger had caught on a briar—at any rate, that the gun had been accidentally discharged."

"They agreed on that, and their official reports severally so stated," Mr. Regan put in. "If it hadn't been for Lon Chambers it would have stayed that way."

"Who is Lon Chambers?" Prescott inquired.

Skinner told him: "The deputy sheriff." His glance shot over June's shoulder at her son. "You're Andrew Dunn, aren't you?"

The young man said he was.

"It was you—you and Miss Fleet—who discovered Hawthorne's body?"

"It was."

"You decided at once that he was dead?"

"Of course. It was obvious."

"You stayed there and sent Miss Fleet to the house to notify your father?"

"She offered to go. She was damn brave." The kid's eyes were truculent and contemptuous as he met the other's gaze, and also his voice. "I told all this to the sheriff and medical examiner, and, as you say, they made notes. Have you read them?"

"I have. Do you object to telling me about it, Mr. Dunn?"

"No. Go ahead."

"Thank you. Before Miss Fleet departed for the house, did you touch or move either the body or the gun?"

"No. She left almost at once."

Skinner's eyes circled. "Did you touch either the body or the gun before you left, Miss Fleet?"

Celia displayed the state of her nerves by saying much louder and more explosively than was necessary, "Of course not!"

"Did you, Mr. Dunn, touch or move either the body or the gun after Miss Fleet left?"

"No."

"How long were you there alone?"

"About fifteen minutes."

"Who came?"

"First my father. He had phoned New City. Stauffer was with him. Then Titus Ames, the man who works there. That was all until the sheriff arrived."

"Were you there, right there on the spot, continuously from the moment you discovered the body until the sheriff arrived?"

"Yes."

"With both the gun and body in full view?"

"The gun wasn't in full view, it was concealed by the briars. I hadn't seen it at all until I looked for it after Miss Fleet left." Andy looked scornful. "If you're trying to establish that neither the gun nor the body was touched by anyone before the sheriff arrived, I can and will testify to it. As a lawyer, I am aware of the proper procedure in cases of death by violence. I am with Dunwoodie, Prescott & Davis."

"I see. A member of the firm?"

"Certainly not. I was admitted to the bar only last year."

"And you can testify as you have stated?"

"Yes. So can my father and the others."

The district attorney's eyes circled again. "Mr. Stauffer? You arrived on the scene with Mr. Dunn, Senior? Do you confirm—"

"Yes," said Stauffer gruffly. "Neither the body nor the gun was touched."

Mr. Regan said, with, it seemed, gloom rather than elation, "That's sewed up."

Skinner nodded. "It seems to be." He looked at Prescott, and then at June. "As you see, Mrs. Dunn, I merely wished to verify some facts. I'll tell you now the basis for my statement a while ago. The sheriff's deputy appears to be an inquisitive and skeptical man. His superiors were for closing the incident as an adventitious tragedy; he was not. Due to his pertinacity the following facts have been established: First, both the stock and barrel of the gun had been recently wiped or rubbed, not by a cloth, as is usual, but by something scratchy that left many tiny streaks, revealed plainly under a magnifying glass. Second, instead of bearing many different fingerprints of Noel Hawthorne's, as a gun should after being carried by a man for more than half an hour, maybe an hour, and fired by him twice, it bore only three sets of his prints, all of the fingers of the right hand—one set on the stock, one on the breechlock, and one on the barrel. The prints were unusual—all four fingers close together, juxtaposed, and none anywhere of the thumb. The set on the barrel was even remarkable, being upside down—that is, not as if the barrel had been grasped in the ordinary manner, but as if it had been held for use as a club, to strike something with the butt."

"This is all poppycock," declared young Dunn scornfully.

Prescott said, "Let him finish, Andy."

"I'll make it as brief as I can," Skinner went on, "but I wish to make it plain that this is merely the inevitable march of events under the guidance of the law. To finish with the fingerprints, they had all been made after the gun had been rubbed with something scratchy. As you doubtless know, Mrs. Dunn, the gun is the property of Titus Ames, who works for you. Ames says it has never been wiped with anything except the soft cloth he uses for that purpose, and that he wiped it with such a cloth Tuesday afternoon, when he went to get it for Mr. Hawthorne at Mr. Dunn's request."

"So you've questioned Ames," Prescott observed.

"I sure have," said Mr. Regan.

Skinner ignored it. "But though Chambers, the deputy, established these facts, he was still unable to convince the sheriff, and the district attorney, Mr. Regan here, that there was ponderable doubt of its having been an accident. In my opinion, that speaks well for the charitable nature of their minds and their disinclination to stir up trouble in the case of so eminent a citizen as Mr. Dunn. However, the sheriff did not forbid his deputy to make further inquiry. On Wednesday, Chambers brought the gun to New York. Thursday, yesterday, our police laboratory reported that there was blood residue, recently deposited, in analyzable quantity, in the crack between the stock and the heelplate, and traces elsewhere. Also yesterday, Chambers found something. A path goes through a corner of the woods, northeast, and at a point it branches, one branch going north to emerge at the edge of the public highway, and the other branch turning east toward your house. Under a shrub near that path, Chambers found a wisp of meadow grass that had been twisted and crushed and apparently used to rub something, and stained in the process. He and Mr. Regan brought it to New York this morning. Four hours ago the laboratory reported that the stains are a mixture of blood and the oily film of the gun, and further, that certain particles which they had previously found on the gun are bits of pollen and fiber from that bunch of grass. Mr. Regan, convinced, consulted me. He told me frankly that on account of the prominence of the persons involved he feared to act. Whatever Miss May Hawthorne may think, it was with reluctance that I accepted his conclusion, and with even greater reluctance that I agreed to help him."

"The conclusion being?" June demanded.

"The obvious and inescapable one, Mrs. Dunn, that your brother was murdered." Skinner met her steady gaze. "If his death was an accident, if he tripped or caught the gun trigger on a briar as was supposed, it is, to put it mildly, difficult to account for the fingerprints. A man doesn't handle a gun that way. And since we have your son's statement, and Mr.

Stauffer's, that the gun wasn't touched after the body
was discovered, there is no possible way, if it was an
accident, to account for the wiping of the gun, the
blood on it, and the wisp of grass. There would be the
same objections to a theory of suicide, were such a
theory advanced. Only on the supposition that it was
murder can these facts be explained. The murderer
shot your brother. He chose not to use his handkerchief, if he had one, to wipe his own fingerprints and a
spot of blood from the gun, but instead plucked a
bunch of grass. Then he printed your brother's fingers
on the gun, using the right hand, and getting them on
the barrel upside down. On his way out through the
woods, he tossed the bunch of grass among some
undergrowth. If he had done that after he reached
the fork instead of before, we would know whether he
was headed for the highway or for your house. As it is,
he bungled badly, either because he figured no crime
would be suspected, or because he was stupid, or
because he feared someone might come and was in great
haste."

"I don't believe it," said April Hawthorne. Everyone looked at her. Her pallor had disappeared, and the
famous ripple was in her voice again. "Not any of it."

Skinner faced her. "What is it you don't believe, Miss
Hawthorne? The facts, or the interpretation of them?"

"I simply don't believe that my brother was murdered. I don't believe that we Hawthornes are having
this happen to us. I don't believe it."

"Neither do I." It was Osric Stauffer backing her
up, energetically.

The district attorney shrugged and returned to
June. "Do you, Mrs. Dunn? I mean, I earnestly want

you to realize that this is what it is, what I said, the cruel and remorseless march of events. I regret it, but I have to deal with it."

June looked at him, said nothing, gave no sign.

"Here," Skinner said, "I want to convince you—I want—I'll have to have—your co-operation in this—and you must understand that your sisters' suspicions, which I suppose you share—are absolutely groundless. No political gossip or slander has anything to do with it. I presume, since you were here consulting him, you regard Nero Wolfe as your friend. He is certainly an expert on crime and evidence." He pivoted. "Mr. Wolfe, is it your opinion that Noel Hawthorne's death was an accident?"

Wolfe shook his head. "I'm an onlooker, Mr. Skinner. I happen to be here because this is my office."

"But your opinion, based on what you have heard?"

"Well . . . am I to accept your facts?"

"Yes. They are unassailable."

"Then they're unique. However, postulating them, Mr. Hawthorne was murdered."

Skinner turned. But by the time he faced June again, she was on her feet. "You can find us at our brother's residence," she told him. "All of us. I shall telephone my husband from there. You'd better come too, Glenn. This means—I know what it means. We'll have to take it." She moved. "Come, Andy. May . . . April, bring Celia . . ."

Wolfe's voice sounded: "If you please, Mrs. Dunn. Do you wish me to proceed with the little matter we were discussing?"

"I think—" Prescott began, but June cut him off:

"Yes. I do. Go ahead. Come, children."

Chapter 5

Wolfe said, "Move closer, Miss Karn, so we won't have to shout. That red chair is the most comfortable."

Naomi Karn, without saying anything, got up, crossed to the red chair, recently vacated by May Hawthorne, and sank into it. She was the only one left. Immediately upon the departure of the Hawthornes and Dunns, with entourage, both branches of law and order had deserted us too. Inspector Cramer, noticing the young woman still inconspicuous in her corner, had pampered his curiosity by firing a question at Wolfe, but Wolfe had waved it off and he had abandoned it and hastened after the others.

Wolfe regarded her with half-closed eyes. After a moment he murmured, "Well. Now you're in a pickle."

She lifted her brows a trifle and asked, "Me? Not at all." She wasn't pasty-faced, as she had been some half an hour before, but she was nothing like as cocky as when she had originally made me sore.

"Oh, yes, you are." Wolfe wiggled a finger at her. "Let's don't start with caracoles. You know very well you're in a devil of a pickle. Those policemen are going up there and ask interminable questions. Among others, about Mr. Hawthorne's will. Even if it's a political foray, which seems doubtful, they'll inquire about the will for the sake of appearances. They always do. Then they'll question you. I expect Inspector Cramer will take that on himself. Mr. Cramer's weapons are nothing remarkable for penetration, but they can do a lot of bruising." He pushed a button. "Will you have some beer?"

She shook her head. "I can't imagine any question anyone could ask me that would be difficult or embarrassing to answer."

"I'll wager that isn't true, Miss Karn. I don't mean merely that there are thousands of questions which I myself would find it difficult or embarrassing to answer, and that doubtless holds for all the members of our race. I mean, specifically, that you were scared half to death when Mr. Skinner announced that Noel Hawthorne was murdered. The confident and defiant intelligence which had flashed from your eyes a moment before, vanished like that." He snapped his fingers. "Also, specifically, what are you here for now?"

"I'm here because you sent for me and I don't intend—"

"No no no. We've turned that page. Mr. Skinner has. That bomb he lugged in here has started a new chapter. It caused a lull, temporary perhaps but complete, in the hostilities over the will; everyone had forgotten all about it until I asked Mrs. Dunn if she wished me to proceed. Including you. If after the shock of Mr. Skinner's announcement, you had resumed thinking about the will, your face would have gone on the warpath again, but it didn't; to this moment it shows only wariness and concern. Your mind isn't on money, Miss Karn, it's on murder, and I have nothing to do with that. Why didn't you get up and go as soon as the others had left? Why did you stay?"

It looked to me as if he had overplayed it, for she wasn't answering him with words, but with action. She had quietly arisen from her chair and started for the door.

Wolfe spoke, with no change in his tone or tempo, to her receding back:

"When your mind leaves murder for money again, let me know and we'll talk it over."

I was feeling disgruntled. Granting that Skinner's bomb had filled the air with fragments, after all the trouble I had taken to bring her there I saw no sense in his shoving her off like that just to hear himself talk. At least I wasn't going to aid and abet by opening doors; I sat. Then I saw her feet were dragging, and with her hand on the knob she stopped and stood there with her back to us. After a few seconds of that she turned abruptly, marched back to the red chair, and sat down.

She looked at Wolfe and said, "I stayed because I was sitting there thinking about something."

He nodded. "Just so," he said pleasantly. "Did you get anywhere?"

"Yes. I did. I made a decision. I was going to tell you what it was, and before I got a chance you jumped on me, about my being in a pickle and being scared half to death. I'm not scared, Mr. Wolfe." Her eyes, leveled at him, certainly didn't look scared, and her voice didn't sound like it. "You can't browbeat me. The last time I was in a panic was when I swallowed a live frog at the age of two. I wouldn't be now, even if I had murdered Mr. Hawthorne myself."

"That's fine. I like spunk. What was the decision you made?"

"I'm not sure I'm going to tell you. I'm not sure but what, after all, it would be better to let it be a fight instead of a compromise."

"Then you haven't really made a decision."

"Yes, I have. And I think—I'll stick to it. I assure you I wasn't frightened into it, but certainly I made it because of this—this news. I'm not in any pickle now, but I have sense enough to know that with the whole Hawthorne gang for bitter enemies I might be. With their position and influence. They can have half the estate. Half of what was left to me."

"Indeed." Wolfe closed his eyes, and after a moment partly opened them again. "So that was your decision."

"It was."

"And you think you'll stick to it."

"I do."

"That's too bad."

"Why is it too bad?"

"Because it's quite likely that if you had made such an offer, say this morning, when Mr. Stauffer called on you, it would have been accepted. Now, unfortunately, it can't be considered. Do you want to hear a counterproposal?"

"What is it?"

"That you get a hundred thousand dollars and my clients get the rest."

Miss Karn got smaller. That was what it looked like, she simply shrank, not back, but in all around. She was smaller. I watched her doing it for ten seconds. But apparently it was only springs coiling tighter inside of her, for all at once she laughed, and it was a pretty good laugh. Then she stopped laughing and said:

"That's *very* funny."

"Oh, no, really, it isn't a bit funny."

"But it is." A sort of chuckle came out of her, like the laugh's colt trotting along behind. "I mean, it's funny that Nero Wolfe should be so utterly mistaken. Such an idiotic blunder for you to make! You must even be fool enough to think I killed Hawthorne myself! That would have been quite a trick, since I was in New York all of Tuesday afternoon."

"I'm not a fool, Miss Karn, and I advise you not to be."

"I'll try not." She arose from her chair and adjusted the blue linen wrap. "Why are you so generous with the hundred thousand? I suppose that's for me to have a good defense lawyer. It's sweet of you, simply darling. Will I find a taxi somewhere?"

"Are you going?"

"Yes. I must. Such a nice party."

"I might be able to persuade my clients to double it. Two hundred thousand. You can reach me here at any time. Taxis are hard to find over here by the river. Mr. Goodwin will take you home. Archie, please stop in the kitchen and tell Saul we'll dine when you return."

I headed off a glance of surprise at him. So the son-of-a-gun had taken steps during my absence uptown. Telling the heiress I'd only be a moment, I left her in the hall and proceeded to the kitchen, and sure enough, there was Saul Panzer playing pinochle for matches with Fred Durkin at my breakfast table. His gray eyes, the best eyes for seeing on the face of the globe, looked up at me sharply.

"Where you bound for?" I asked him. "Tail on a woman named Karn?"

"Yes."

"She's off. I'm taking her home. 787 Park Avenue, 12D. It's just possible she'll ask me to let her out before we get there. You got a car? Good. I'll take it easy. Across 34th to Park and then uptown. If you get close to her, lash yourself to the mast and count ten. Her middle name is Delilah."

I went back to the hall and got her and escorted her to the roadster. She made no effort at small talk as I took my time going crosstown on 34th, dawdling until I caught sight, in the driving mirror, of Saul's coupé only two cars back. I was thinking what a come down. On the trip bringing her to Wolfe's house I had had seven million bucks there on the seat with me, and now going back apparently all I had was a measly hundred thousand, or at the most twice that. It was no wonder she didn't feel like talking, after that amount of deflation. She did manage to murmur thanks when I delivered her on the sidewalk in front of her address. Saul had rounded the corner into 73rd, for a parking space. I inspected a wheel until he was in sight again, and then remounted and applied the spur.

I got back home at 8:30, and was touched to find

that Wolfe had waited dinner for me, our usual hour
being eight o'clock. Fred Durkin was still around at a
dollar an hour, which surprised me, since Wolfe wasn't
the kind of man to take expensive precautions when
the treasury was plucking at the counterpane. If it had
been Saul Panzer or Orrie Cather, he would have
eaten with Wolfe and me, but since it was Fred he ate
in the kitchen with Fritz. Fred put vinegar on things,
and no man who did that ate at Wolfe's table. Fred did
it back in 1932, calling for vinegar and stirring it into
brown roux for a squab. Nothing had been said, Wolfe
regarding it as immoral to interfere with anybody's
meal until it was down and the digestive processes
completed, but the next morning he had fired Fred
and kept him fired for over a month.

After dinner we wandered back into the office.
Wolfe got himself settled at his desk with the atlas,
and I indulged in a grin when I saw that instead of
departing for a little journey to Outer Mongolia he had
turned to the map of New York Sate and, judging
from the slant of his eyes, was freshening up on
Rockland County. I had just selected a book for a quiet
hour when the phone rang. I got to my instrument and
told the transmitter:

"Office of Nero Wolfe."

Hearing my name in a familiar voice, I told Wolfe
it was Saul Panzer, and with a sigh he put the atlas
down and took it on his extension, and grunted a green
light.

"9:56, sir," Saul's voice said. "Subject entered
apartment house, delivered by Archie, at 8:14. At 9:12
she came out again, took a taxi to Santoretti's, Italian
restaurant at 833 East 62nd Street, and went in. I

went in and ate spaghetti and talked Italian with the
waiter. She is there at a table with a man, eating
chicken and mushrooms. He has no appetite, but she
has. They talk in undertones. I'm phoning from a
drugstore at the northwest corner of 62nd and Second
Avenue. If they separate after leaving, which one do I
take?"

"Describe the man."

"40 to 45, 5 feet 10, 170 pounds. Drinks. Suit,
well-made gray tropical worsted, hat expensive flop-
brim gray summer-weight felt. Shaved yesterday.
Blue shirt, gray four-in-hand with blue stripe.
Medium-square jaw, wide mouth and full lips, long
narrow nose, puffy around the eyes, brown eyes with
a nervous blink, ears set—"

"That will do. You don't know him."

"No, sir." Saul was apologetic at having to report a
man for whom he had no entry in the extensive and
accurate card index he carried in his skull.

Wolfe said, "Fred will join you across the street
from Santoretti's as soon as possible. If they separate,
give him the man. That woman could be difficult."

"Yes, sir, I agree."

Wolfe hung up and tossed me a nod, and I went to
the kitchen, where I interrupted Fred in the middle of
a yawn that would have held a quart of vinegar. I gave
him the picture, told him it was a till further notice,
with emphasis on identity, and herded his ungainly
bulk through the hall and out the front door. Standing
out on the stone stoop for a breath of nice hot July air,
watching him hotfoot it for the corner, I observed a
taxi zooming along in my direction, heard the brakes
screech, and saw it stop with a jerk at the curb below

me. A woman got out, paid the driver and dismissed him, crossed the sidewalk and mounted the seven steps, and smiled sweetly at me in the light that came through the open door.

"May I see Mr. Wolfe?"

I nodded hospitably and ushered her into the hall, asked her to wait a minute, and went to the office and told Wolfe that Miss May Hawthorne requested an audience.

Chapter 6

The office had been restored to its normal condition as to chairs. As usual, the red one was at the right of Wolfe's desk, turned to face him, and the college president sat in it. She looked tired and her eyes had little red streaks on the whites, but her backbone wasn't sagging.

Wolfe said, "That was quite a shock you folks got here this afternoon."

She nodded. "It's hard on us. Especially on my sister April, because she pretends she has to laugh at everything. Art making faces at life. Have you had a talk with Miss Karn?"

"A short one. She stayed after the others left."

"Did you make an agreement with her?"

"No. She offered to relinquish half of the estate, but I refused that."

"Thank goodness." Miss Hawthorne looked relieved. "Knowing your reputation, and having had a look at you, I was afraid you might have cornered her and got us committed. But you realize, of course, that the situation is entirely changed. In my opinion, it is now inadvisable to deal with her at all."

"Indeed. Do the others agree with you?"

"I don't know. I believe they will. The point is this, we wished to come to an arrangement with Miss Karn as soon as possible to avoid the fracas my sister-in-law was determined to start. Now it doesn't matter. With the soot a murder investigation will deposit all over us, a will contest wouldn't even make a smudge."

Wolfe pursed his lips. "That's one way of looking at it. I suppose Mr. Skinner and the others followed you people home?"

"Certainly they did. My sister-in-law had them admitted, but on Mr. Prescott's advice we all—all but Daisy—refused to see them until my sister June had phoned her husband in Washington. He told her we should assist the authorities all we could by answering any relevant questions. Then they went after us—oh, I suppose they were considerate and courteous. The result seems to be that we are all suspected of murder."

"All?"

"Most of us. I presume that sort of nightmare is familiar enough to you, but I am not a detective and I don't read crime stories in the papers, I'm too busy. Apparently my brother died—was shot—between 4:30 and 5:30. Titus Ames heard a third shot a little before five o'clock—there had been two previous ones which dead crows account for. At that time my sister April was upstairs taking a nap, but no one was there watching her. My sister was somewhere picking raspberries and grape leaves for a table decoration. I was in a bathroom washing stockings."

I thought, aha, the magazine was right, she really does! She was going on:

"Celia—Miss Fleet—was in her room writing letters. She answers all the letters from morons my sister April receives. Mrs. Ames was making preparations for the dinner. Daisy, Noel's wife, was out in a meadow picking blackeyed susans. She calls them daisies. John—my brother-in-law—was chopping wood. Those men actually asked me, very courteously, if I remember hearing his axe going all the time I was washing stockings. I washed my hair too. Mr. Stauffer, whom I violently dislike, had gone to the pond for a swim. Titus Ames was milking cows. Andy had driven to Nyack to get some ice cream, but that doesn't clear him, because the highway passes not far from where it happened, just the other side of a strip of woods. Sara and Mr. Prescott were in New York and didn't get there until half past seven, nearly two hours after my brother's body was found—Mr. Prescott drove Sara out in his car—but I shouldn't think they're out of it either—couldn't one of them have come previously in an airplane and gone back again?"

Wolfe nodded gravely. "Or even a glider from the Empire State Building; it's only thirty or forty miles. Since it's already fantastic, we might as well pile it on."

"It's not fantastic at all," Miss Hawthorne retorted. "It's cold and horrible fact. And they're going to work on it. They're going to proceed on the theory that my brother was murdered because he had John Dunn's career in his grip and wouldn't let go. They can't move anything—that is, they can't convict anyone of murder—but they can ruin John, and they will—"

She pressed her palm to her forehead and closed her eyes.

Wolfe murmured, "A little brandy, Archie."

I got up to get it, but she shook her head and said, "No." I hesitated. She said, "No thanks, really," and dropped her hand and opened her eyes at Wolfe.

She straightened her back. "I beg your pardon. I didn't intend—I only spoke of all that to explain why I think you shouldn't go ahead with Miss Karn. We no longer shrink from scandal and sensation. I have no rancor for Miss Karn, but there is no reason she should get anything my brother didn't intend her to get. I don't believe that that grotesque paper Mr. Prescott read to us expresses my brother's intentions at all. Noel had faults, plenty of them, but he told me he was bequeathing a million dollars to the Varney science fund, and nothing will ever convince me that he didn't do it."

"You said that this afternoon."

"I repeat it."

"Then you accuse Mr. Prescott of villainy. He drew the will and produces this one as authentic. Do you think he is splitting with Miss Karn?"

"Good heavens, no." Her eyes widened in astonishment.

Wolfe frowned. "I'm afraid your mind isn't working very well, Miss Hawthorne. No wonder, with the jolts you've had. You say you believe—when did your brother tell you he was leaving a million to your fund?"

"He mentioned it two or three times. A year ago last winter he informed me he intended to make it a million instead of half that amount. Last summer he told me he had done so."

"The summer of 1938?"

"Yes."

"Well. You say you are convinced he wasn't deceiving you. That he had done what he said. But the will which Mr. Prescott presents as authentic is dated March 7th, 1938, and it was after that date that your brother told you he had changed it to a million for your fund. Therefore you are charging Mr. Prescott with fraud."

"Not at all," she declared impatiently. "If I had to base my contention on a supposition as improbable as that, I'd abandon it. I know Glenn Prescott. He's a fairly shrewd and capable Wall Street lawyer, with the natural flexibility in ethics and morals that is a functional necessity in his environment, but he totally lacks the daring and imagination that are required for banditry in the grand manner. I would be as likely to write a great epic poem as he would be to steal three million dollars by substituting a forgery for my brother's will. I suppose that's what you meant—that about his splitting with Miss Karn."

"Roughly, yes. Some degree of forgery. Not necessarily counterfeiting signatures. Have you seen the document?"

"Yes."

"Is it all on one page?"

"No. Two."

"Typewritten, of course?"

"Yes."

"Are any of the main provisions on page two?"

She frowned. "I don't— Wait. Yes, I do. Most of the typed matter is on page one. A little on page two, and of course the signatures—my brother's and the witnesses'."

"Then it might not have been necessary to attempt the hazardous process of forging signatures. But if you rule out fraud on the part of Prescott, on what ground can you contend—"

"I was coming to it. That's what I came to tell you. I think it happened like this. Noel did have Prescott draw that will for him, just as it is now, and keep it in his office vault. But at the same time, or rather a little later, perhaps the next day, Noel superseded it by drawing another will, himself, without Prescott's knowledge, which disposed of his fortune as he did in fact desire to dispose of it. The question is, where is the last will? The only valid one?"

Wolfe grunted. "There seems to be a prior question. Why did your brother have Mr. Prescott draw a will which he intended so promptly to supersede? So much trouble."

May shook her head. "Not much, since he had to. Prescott himself furnished the hint for that. We asked him last night if Miss Karn knew about the will, and he said yes. He said that the day after it was drawn Miss Karn saw the will and read it through. She went to Prescott's office—the appointment was made by Noel, and Noel instructed Prescott to show her the will."

"I see," Wolfe murmured.

"So that answers your question." A faint, almost imperceptible tinge of color appeared in the college president's cheeks. "I don't pretend to know anything about sex and what it does to people. There is very little else about men and women that I don't understand fairly well, but I confess that sex is beyond me.

It missed me, or perhaps I dodged it. I have my college, my achievement, my career, I have myself. It is only by a rational process, not by any emotional comprehension, that it becomes intelligible to me that my brother descended to such trickery. He wished to keep his word to me and to fulfill his obligations to others. But he had to have Miss Karn, and he could keep her only by showing her that if he died she would get her—reward. I admit that I am incapable of understanding why he had to have Miss Karn specifically, with so fierce a necessity, but there are thousands of experts, from Shakespeare to Faith Baldwin, to back me up."

Wolfe nodded. "We won't quarrel about that. It's a neat theory you've built up. Is it yours exclusively?"

"I contrived it. My sisters incline to it. Mr. Prescott weakly contends that Noel was above such a trick, but I think he secretly agrees with me. I suspect he knows as little about sex as I do. He has never married."

"Are you here as a representative of the group who hired me to negotiate with Miss Karn?"

"Yes. That is, my sisters—not my sister-in-law, Daisy. She won't talk sense. The fact is, they're in such a state about the—development regarding my brother's death—that the will doesn't matter to them. It does to me. My brother is dead. We have buried him. He desired and intended that in the unhappy event of his death, my college should benefit. I am going to see to it that his intention is fulfilled. With my sisters' acquiescence—we want you to postpone the negotiations with Miss Karn—"

"I have offered to let her keep two hundred thousand dollars, the remainder to be divided by Mrs. Hawthorne and the rest of you."

May gawked at him. "You don't mean she accepted that offer?"

"No. But she may—tomorrow, any time. She's scared."

"What's she scared about?"

"Murder. A murder investigation is a whirlpool of menace, Miss Hawthorne. I confess it doesn't seem to have frightened you very much."

"I'm tough. The Hawthorne girls are all tough. But damn it, do you mean Miss Karn murdered Noel herself?" She was still gawking. "My mind was so— that never occurred to me!"

"I have no idea who murdered your brother. Let's stick to the will. I was only explaining Miss Karn's fright. In spite of your interesting theory, and granting that it's sound and even correct, if Miss Karn accepts my offer I shall execute an agreement and have her sign it, and I shall advise you people to sign it also."

"She won't accept it."

"I speak of a contingency."

"Which we'll meet if it arises." She matched his crispness. "What I came here for, and it's taken me long enough to get to it, was to ask you to find my brother's will. The last one, the real one. If it gives anything to Miss Karn, she's welcome to it."

Wolfe shook his head. "I was afraid you were going to say that. I'm not a ferret, madam. I can't undertake it."

That started a wrangle. It lasted for a quarter of

an hour, and got nowhere. Wolfe's position was that it would be farcical for him to try such a job, since he didn't have access to the various buildings, offices, dwellings, rooms and enclosures in which Noel Hawthorne might have deposited the will, that to gain such access through the authority of the executor of the estate, the Cosmopolitan Trust Company, would be difficult if not impossible, and that if there was such a will it would be found in good time by the persons who went through the dead man's papers. May contended that detectives were supposed to find things and that he was a detective.

It came out a tie. Like the man trying to pull up an oak tree who finally quit and muttered, "You can't pull me up, either." Miss Hawthorne didn't actually mutter as she got up and walked out of the office, but she wasn't admitting she was licked, either by her words or the expression of her face. I let her into the hall, and wasn't sorry when she accepted my offer to drive her home, since it meant a breath of cooler midnight air. She took off her hat, stuck her chin out, closed her eyes, and let her hair fly as we rolled up Fifth Avenue. The Hawthorne residence on 67th Street, which I eyed with moderate curiosity as I drew up in front, was a big old gray stone four-storied affair with iron grills on the windows, a few doors east of Fifth. May smiled sweetly when she thanked me and said good night.

Back home, I went to the kitchen and snared a glass of milk before proceeding to the office. Wolfe had just finished number two of a pair of beer bottles. I stood sipping milk and looking down at him approvingly. The milk was a little too cold and I took my time sipping.

"Stop smirking!" he yapped.

"Hell, I'm not smirking." I lowered the back of my lap to the edge of a chair. "I think you're wonderful. The things you put up with to keep Fritz and Theodore and me off of relief! What do you think of the famous Hawthrone girls?"

He grunted.

"The murder part of it," I declared, "is a cinch. Titus Ames did it because he wants to dress up like a girl himself and go to Varney College and study science, and on account of loyalty to the alma mater he's going to have he killed Noel so the science fund would get the million. Now May's furious because the million has shrunk to a tithe of its former self, and with a daring imagination she sells you a fairy tale about a secret will hid in a hollow tree and that kind of crap—"

"She sold me nothing. Go to bed."

"Do you give credence to her theory about the second will?"

He put his hands on the rim of the desk, getting ready to push his chair back, and seeing that I beat him to it by arising and striding from the scene. I kept on going, up two flights of stairs, to my own room. There, after finishing the milk, I undraped my form, shaved my legs and removed my eyelashes, and dropped languorously into the arms of the sandman.

When I rolled out at eight in the morning it was tuning up for another hot one. The air coming in at the window made you gasp for more when what you really wanted was less. So I kept the shower moderately cool and selected a palm beach for the day's apparel. Down in the kitchen Fritz was puffing, having just returned from delivering Wolfe's breakfast tray to his room on the second floor. Glancing over the *Times* as I sat negotiating with my orange juice and eggs and rolls, I found no indication that Skinner, Cramer & Co., had opened the big bag of news regarding the death of Noel Hawthorne; there wasn't any hint of it. Apparently they realized it was going to be a busy intersection and were taking no chances. I poured my second cup of coffee and turned to the sports page, and the phone rang.

I took it there in the kitchen, on Fritz's extension, and got Fred Durkin's voice in my ear, in an urgent kind of a whisper that gave me the idea he had stepped on somebody's foot and got arrested again.

"Archie?"

"Me talking."

"You'd better come up here right away."

Then I was sure of it, I asked wearily, "Which precinct?"

"No, listen. Come on up here. 913 West 11th, an old brownstone. I'm here and I'm not supposed to be. Push the button under Dawson and up two flights. I'll let you in."

"What the hell kind of a—"

"You come on, and step on it."

The connection clicked off. I said something expressive. Fritz giggled, and I threw a roll at him which he caught with one hand and threw back, but missed me. I had to gulp the coffee, and it was as hot as hell's dishwater. Giving Fritz a message for Wolfe, I stopped in at the office for my shoulder strap and automatic just in case, trotted a block to the garage to get the roadster, and headed downtown.

But nobody got shot. I parked a hundred feet east of the number on 11th Street, mounted the stoop to the old-fashioned vestibule, punched the button under Earl Dawson, pushed through when the click came, and went up two flights of narrow dark stairs. A door at the end of the hall opened cautiously and gave me a glimpse of Fred's map of Ireland. I walked to it, shoved it open and went in, and closed it again.

Fred whispered, "Jesus, I didn't know what to do."

I glanced around. It was a big room with nice rugs on a polished floor and comfortable chairs and so forth. No inhabitants were in sight.

"Lovely place you've got," I observed. "It would look better—"

"Shut up," Fred hissed. He was making for a door to an inner room and crooking a finger at me. "Come here and look."

I followed him through the door. This room was smaller, with another nice rug, a couple of chairs, a dressing table, a chest of drawers, and a big fine-looking bed. I focused my gaze on the man who was lying on the bed, and saw that he checked with the description Saul had given of the item Naomi Karn had met at Santoretti's, in spite of a couple of missing details. The blue shirt, gray four-in-hand, and gray tropical worsted coat were there on him, but below them was only white drawers, bare legs, and blue socks and garters. He was breathing like a geyser getting ready to shoot.

Fred, looking down at him proudly, whispered, "He groaned when I pulled his pants off, so I quit."

I nodded. "He don't look very dignified. Have you named him yet?"

"Yeah, but it's a mix-up. It says Dawson downstairs, and this is where he said to bring him, and he had keys, but that's not his name. His name's Eugene Davis, and he's in a law firm; Dunwoodie, Prescott & Davis, 40 Broadway."

Chapter 7

I gave Fred an eye. The comic aspect of things retreated into the wings.

"What makes you think so?" I demanded.

"I frisked him. Look there on the dresser."

I tiptoed across to inspect the little heap of articles. Among other things, a driving license for Eugene Davis. A membership card in the New York County Bar Association for Eugene Davis, of Dunwoodie, Prescott & Davis. A pass to the New York World's Fair 1939, with a picture of him thereon. An accident insurance identification card. Three letters received by Eugene Davis at his business address. Two snapshots of Naomi Karn, one in a bathing suit. . . .

I told Fred, "Go and stay at the hall door and scream if anyone comes. I'm going to browse around."

I made it snappy but thorough. Davis lay there sucking it in like a bear caught short on Atmosphere common. I covered it all, that bedroom and a smaller one, bathroom, kitchenette, and the big living room, including closets. I would have floated right out of a window if I had found a last will and testament of Noel

Hawthorne dated subsequent to March 7th, 1938, but I didn't. Nor anything else that seemed pertinent to a will or a murder or any phenomenon I was interested in, unless you want to count eight more pictures of Naomi Karn, of various shapes and sizes, three of them inscribed "To Gene," with dates in 1935 and 1936. Even the refrigerator was empty. I took a parting look at the member of the bar, collected Fred and escorted him out and down to the street and into the roadster, drove around the corner onto Sixth Avenue, drew up at the curb in the morning shadow of the buildings, and demanded:

"How come?"

Fred protested, "We ought to park where we can see—"

"He'll be there for hours. Tell Papa."

"Well, I tailed him—"

"Did he and the female subject leave Santoretti's together?"

"Yeah, at eleven o'clock. They walked west to Lexington, with me on foot and Saul stringing along in his bus. He put her in a taxi and Saul followed it. He stood and watched the taxi, going uptown, until it was out of sight, and then he started walking south as if he'd just remembered something he'd left in Florida. He's a giraffe. I damn near ran my legs off. The damn fool walked clear to 8th Street!"

"We'll warn him not to do that again. How you must have suffered. Skip things like that. I can't bear it."

"Go spit up a rope. He went into a place on 8th Street near Sixth, a bar and restaurant named Wellman's. I happen to know a guy that works there. I

waited outside a while, and then I went in and saw
that Sam was there filling and spilling—he's the guy I
know. I bought a drink and chinned with him. The
subject was there at the bar taking on cargo. He
would sip at one maybe ten minutes and then down it
would go and he'd get a refill. After that had been
going on for an hour and a half Sam began frowning at
him and I asked Sam about him. By the way, I had to
turn loose of two dollars and sixty cents for refreshments."

"I'll bet you did. Wait till Wolfe sees the expense
account, I won't pass it."

"Now, look here, Archie—"

"I'll see. Finish your report to your superior."

"Wait till I laugh. Haw. Sam said the subject was a
good customer, too damn good sometimes. His name
was Dawson and he lived in the neighborhood. A
dozen times in the past two years Sam had had to get
him home in a taxi. Well, it went on and on. After a
while he staggered over to a table and sat down and
asked for more. Finally he flopped. Sam and I made a
couple of efforts to straighten him up, but he was out.
So I offered to see him home, and Sam thought that
was swell of me, and so did I until I started carrying
him up that two flights of stairs. He weighs two
hundred if he weighs an ounce."

"Saul says a hundred and seventy."

"Saul didn't carry him upstairs. It was a quarter
after five when I got him here. I took his pants and
shoes off, and then sat and thought it over. The main
thing was, why should I get you out of bed at that
hour? I know how you are before breakfast—"

"So you took a nap and then phoned an SOS as if—"

"I didn't take a nap. I just wanted you to realize—"

"Okay. Save it. I may as well admit that the boss will pay for the drinks. I also admit it's handy your knowing so many Sams in so many bars. I'll be back pretty soon."

I hopped out, went to the corner and entered a drugstore, found a phone booth, and dialed a number. A familiar voice said hello.

"This is Archie, Fritz. Give the plant rooms a buzz."

"Mr. Wolfe isn't up there."

I glanced at my wrist watch and saw 10:05. "What are you talking about? Certainly he's up there."

"No, really, Archie. Mr. Wolfe has gone out."

"You're crazy. If he told you to say that—who does he think he's kidding, anyhow? Ring the plant rooms."

"But, Archie, I tell you he went. He received a telephone call and went. He gave me messages for you—wait—I wrote them down—First, Saul reported and he arranged to have Orrie relieve him. Second, that owing to your absence he would have to ride in a taxicab. Third, that you are to go in the sedan to the residence of Mr. Hawthorne, deceased, on 67th Street."

"Is this straight, Fritz?"

"Honest for God, Archie. It took my breath."

"I'll bet it did."

I hung up and went back out to the car and told Fred:

"A new era has begun. The earth has turned around and started the other way. Mr. Wolfe has left home in a taxicab to work on a case."

"Huh? Nuts."

"Nope. As Fritz says, honest for God. He really has. So if you'll—"

"But Jesus, Archie. He'll get killed or something."

"Don't I know it? You beat it. Go on home and finish your nap. Your friend Davis is set for several hours at least. If we need you I'll give you a ring."

"But if Mr. Wolfe—"

"I'll tend to him."

He climbed out and stood there shaking his head and looking worried as I drove off. I wasn't worried, but I was slightly dazed, as I headed the roadster north. Arriving at the garage on Eleventh Avenue, I transferred to the sedan, circled down the ramp to the street, and started north again. I figured that it must be the state of the bank account that was responsible for Wolfe's shattering his inflexible rule never to go calling on business, but though I knew he was concerned about it I hadn't realized that he was in a condition of absolute frenzy. I was feeling pretty sorry for him as I parked the sedan on 67th Street and walked to the entrance of the Hawthorne stone pile.

There were no city employees standing around and no reporters or photographers climbing in at the windows, so I concluded that Skinner and Cramer still hadn't blown the horn for the busy intersection. The butler who opened the door had distinguished ancestry oozing from every pore. I said:

"Good morning, Jeeves. I'm Lord Goodwin. If Mr. Nero Wolfe got here alive, he's expecting me. A big fat man. Is he here?"

"Yes, sir." He permitted me to slide through. "Your hat, sir? This way if you please, sir." He moved across the large entrance hall to a doorway and stood aside for me. "I shall inform Mr. Dunn and Mr. Wolfe that you are here." I sauntered by him with a nod and he went off.

So that was why Wolfe was zooming around like a wren building a nest. It would have been more pat to our purpose if it had been the secretary of the treasury instead of the secretary of state, but you can't have a silver lining without a cloud. I shrugged it off and glanced around. With all its size and elegant and successful effort to live up to the butler, the room was not what I would live in if my rich uncle died. There were too many chairs that looked as if they had been made to have their pictures taken instead of to sit on. The only thing I saw that I liked was a marble statue over in a corner of a woman reaching for a bath towel—at least she had an arm stretched as if she was reaching for something, and she was ready for a towel. I strolled across to appreciate it, and, as I stood doing so, got a certain feeling in the back of my neck, though I hadn't heard a sound. I whirled on my heel, and saw what had caused it. Mrs. Noel Hawthorne was there at the other end of the room, facing me. That is, she would have been facing me if she had had a face. She had on a long gray dress that reached to her ankles, and the veil was the same gray. She just stood there.

I was certainly allergic to that damn veil. There was something about it that was bad for my nerves. I wanted to say, "Good morning, Mrs. Hawthorne," with my customary suavity, but had the feeling it would come out a yell, so I said nothing. Neither did she. After she had stood there an hour, which I suppose was actually nine seconds, she turned and, noiselessly on the thick carpet, disappeared the other side of some draperies. I strode across the room as if I was going to do something; I suppose if I had had my sword handy I would have lunged through the drapery with it like Hamlet in the third act. Before I got there a voice from the rear stopped me:

"Hullo!"

I jerked around like Gary Cooper surrounded by cutthroats, saw who it was and felt like a fool, and blurted savagely, "Hullo yourself!"

Sara Dunn, the professional fiend, approached. "I forget your name. I suppose you're going to sit in with Nero Wolfe and my dad?"

"I guess I am if I live long enough."

She was in front of me, looking up at me with her mother's fighting bird eyes. "Will you do something for me? Tell Nero Wolfe I want to see him before he leaves here. As soon as possible. Tell him so my dad can't hear."

"I'll try. You might save time by telling me what you want to see him about."

"I don't know." Her brow wrinkled. "Maybe I should. It's something I'd like him to know—"

She turned at a noise. The butler was coming through the doorway.

"Yes, Turner?"

"I beg your pardon, Miss Dunn. Your father is expecting Mr. Goodwin upstairs."

"They can wait a minute," I said, "if you want—"

She shook her head. "No, it would be—tell him what I said. Will you?"

I said I would, and followed the butler. From the entrance hall he mounted a wide curving stairway, and in the upper corridor passed one door on the right and opened the second one. I went in. A glance showed me that this room was closer to my idea of what to do to keep in out of the rain if you have money. There were shelves with books on three sides, pictures of horses and dogs, a big roomy flat-top desk, plenty of comfortable chairs, and a radio. No one was at the desk. Nero Wolfe was holding down a brown leather chair with his back to a window. Mrs. John Charles Dunn was on the edge of another one. Standing between them was a tall stoop-shouldered guy in shirt sleeves, with harassed deep-set eyes and a wavy mane of hair turning gray. I would have recognized him immediately from pictures I had seen, and of course he was noted for shedding his coat and vest whenever circumstances permitted.

Wolfe grunted a greeting. June murmured at me and introduced me to her husband. Wolfe said:

"Sit down, Archie. I have explained your function to Mr. and Mrs. Dunn. Did Fred get into trouble again?"

"No, sir, I wouldn't say trouble. Following the instructions I gave him, he walked around and sat in a bar having refreshments until five o'clock. Then one of the bar's customers needed to be conveyed home and Fred obliged. I joined him in the customer's apartment at the address I told Fritz to give you, arriving at nine o'clock. The customer was on the bed in a coma sequential to acute inebriation. After looking around to make sure that everything was all right, I departed, phoned the house, and received your message from Fritz. Fred has gone home to sleep."

"The customer's identity?"

"Yes, sir."

"Well?"

I shrugged. If the lid was off for the cabinet member and wife, okay. "Eugene Davis, of the law firm of Dunwoodie, Prescott & Davis."

"Ah."

Mrs. Dunn asked in a tone of surprise, "Gene Davis?"

"Do you know him, madam?" inquired Wolfe.

"Not well. I haven't seen him for a long time." She turned to her husband. "You remember him, John. Eugene Davis, Glenn's partner. I don't think either of us has seen him since we went to Washington."

Dunn nodded uncertainly. "I believe I do. A fellow with a narrow nose and too much blood in his lips. But he has no connection with this—has he? Eugene Davis?"

"I don't know," Wolfe said. "Anyway, he is at present in a drunken stupor, so he'll keep. You were saying, sir? . . ."

"Yes." Dunn scowled at me and then transferred it to Wolfe. "I don't like this man's being here, but what I like is no longer of much significance." He sounded bitter.

"I wouldn't say that," Wolfe remonstrated. "I've explained about Mr. Goodwin. Without him I'm an ear without a tympanum. Go ahead. You made a fine dramatic statement, which pleased me very much because I'm an incurable romantic. You said you are going to put your fate in my hands."

"There was nothing dramatic about it. It was merely a statement of fact."

"I like facts too."

"I don't," Dunn muttered. "Not these facts." He

turned and looked at his wife, then abruptly went over to her and bent down to kiss her on the lips. "June dear," he said. "I've hardly even said hello to you. June dear." She pulled him back down and had him kiss her again and muttered at him. Wolfe told me:

"Mr. Dunn just arrived from Washington. He phoned me from the airport."

Dunn straightened up and came back to Wolfe. "You've heard the report that is being spread about Noel Hawthorne and me."

Wolfe nodded. "Something, yes, sir. The editor of the *Gazette* dines with me once a month. That the decision to make the loan to Argentina was arrived at in the State Department. That shortly after the loan was announced, it was learned that valuable industrial concessions in Argentina had already been secured by companies controlled by Daniel Cullen and Company. That Noel Hawthorne had, through you, his brother-in-law, received prior secret information of the loan and its terms. That you, the secretary of state, are as good as convicted of skulduggery."

"Do you believe it?"

"I know nothing whatever about it."

"It's a damned lie. If you believe it, you are disqualified for what I want you to do."

"I have no basis for belief or disbelief. I don't try to abolish reality by shutting my eyes, nor do I gobble garbage. As a citizen, I like your methods and approve your policies. I am a professional detective, and if I take a job I work at it. What do you want me to do?"

"You did a brilliant piece of work on the Wetzler case."

"Thank you, sir. What do you want me to do?"

"I want you to find out who murdered Noel Hawthorne."

"Indeed." Wolfe heaved a sigh. I looked across at June and saw that her fingers were twisted tight in her lap as she gazed across at her husband. Dunn, standing in front of Wolfe, scowled down at him.

"My career is ruined anyhow," he declared. "My wife's too, for it has been as much hers as mine. I'll probably have to resign within a month. I'll clear it up some day, the question of how the Cullen office got that advance information. My brother-in-law claimed he didn't know. I'll do that before I die, in spite of the intrigue and obscurities and obstacles. But the first thing to clear up is this murder." Dunn clenched his fists. "By God, I won't leave Washington with this on my shoulders too."

Wolfe grunted. "Miss May Hawthorne seems to think that your political opponents are deliberately using Hawthorne's death as a lever to pry you out. Do you?"

"I don't know. I make no such charge. But I do know that if the murder is not solved I'll never crawl out of the mire, either before my death or after, and I don't think they'll solve it. I don't believe they will." Dunn's fists closed again. "I suppose this Argentina thing has worn my nerves thin and they're ready to snap, but I don't trust anybody. Not anybody. People who sit at the same table with me at a cabinet meeting will help tear my scalp off. Am I going to trust my life—more than my life—to a Rockland County district attorney or a slick rabble-rouser like Bill Skinner? I am not! There's not a soul in Washington that I can trust who is in a position to help me in a thing like this. And people don't like to help a man who is supposed to be going down for the third time, not even when—especially when—he occupies a position like mine. I need you, Mr. Wolfe. I want you to find out who killed Hawthorne."

"Well." Wolfe stirred in his chair. "I have already accepted a commission—"

"I know you have. But first another thing. My salary is $15,000 a year and I have a hard time living on it. If I resign and resume private practice—"

Wolfe waved it away. "If you can trust me with your fate I can trust you for a fee. But I can't undertake to look two ways at once. Your wife and her sisters and Mrs. Hawthorne have engaged me in the matter of the will. They are my clients. If I take on your job too I run the risk of finding myself confronted by the painful necessity . . ."

Wolfe let it hang. Dunn glowered at him. The tableau was interrupted by a knock at the door, followed by its opening for the entrance of the butler.

"What is it?" Dunn demanded.

"Three gentlemen to see you, sir. Mr. Skinner, Mr. Cramer and Mr. Hombert."

"Ask them to wait. Tell them—put them in that room with the piano. I'll see them there."

The butler bowed and went. June, looking across at Wolfe, said quietly, "You mean, what if one of us killed my brother."

"Bosh!" Dunn blurted.

June shook her head at him. "Bosh to us, John, not to Mr. Wolfe." Her eyes went to Wolfe. "If we ask you to expose a murderer, we'll expect you to do so if you can. Do you really—do you think one of us did it?"

"I haven't started thinking," said Wolfe testily. "I just want things understood. I don't like it. If Miss May Hawthorne, for instance, is going to be convicted for murder, I'd rather have nothing to do with it. I work as a detective to make money, and I expect to make some on that will business. I'd prefer to let it go at that, but my confounded vanity won't let me. John Charles Dunn stands here and puts his fate in my hands. What the devil is a conceited man like me going to do?" He frowned at Dunn. "I warn you, sir, that if I start after this murderer I'm apt to catch him. Or her."

"I hope you do."

"So do I," said June. "We all do."

"Except one of you," said Wolfe grimly. "At present I know nothing at all about it, but if Mr. Skinner is proceeding on the theory that Hawthorne was killed by someone in that gathering at your house, I don't blame him. At any rate, I'll have to start with them. Separately. Who is on the premises?"

"My sisters are," said June. "and the children, and I think Miss Fleet . . ."

I chimed in, "I saw Mrs. Hawthorne downstairs, or at least someone in a veil."

"That will do to begin with," said Wolfe. "You, Mr. Dunn? It won't hurt Mr. Skinner to wait a few minutes longer. I understand you were chopping wood. Miss May Hawthorne says she was asked whether she heard your axe going continuously from 4:30 to 5:30."

"She didn't," Dunn said curtly. "I'm not a robot. I sat on a log. I was in a stew. I didn't like Noel Hawthorne being there, even for our anniversary."

"It wasn't exactly a gay carefree party."

"It was not."

"Around four o'clock you and Hawthorne had discussed shooting a hawk?"

"The hawk was there, flying around, over towards the woods. Ames had told me it had got a chicken the day before, and I told Noel. He wanted to shoot it. He liked to shoot things. I don't. I found Ames and told him to give Noel his shotgun, and Noel went off with it. I went the other way, around back of the sheds, to let off steam splitting wood."

"Did Hawthorne himself suggest shooting the hawk? Or did you suggest it to get rid of him?"

"He suggested it." Dunn was frowning. "See here. You'd better put me at the end of the list. I'm aware what you're capable of, and I don't swagger. It wouldn't be in me to put you on this as a finesse if my own heel was exposed."

"But it's my job now, Mr. Dunn. Were others present when the hawk was discussed?"

"Yes, we were having tea on the lawn. Most of us."

"Then I can ask them. Even if there were something to fish out of you, I doubt if I could do it; you've had long training. Do you know of anything that happened that afternoon that you think might help me? Anything at all?"

"No. Nothing is in my mind now."

"Do you suspect anyone of murdering Hawthorne?"

"Yes, I suspect his wife. His widow."

"Indeed." Wolfe's brows went up. "Any special reason?"

"That's just leaping in the dark, John," June remonstrated. "Poor Daisy is a spiteful wretch, but—"

"I answered his question, June dear. He asked if I suspect anyone—No special reason, Mr. Wolfe. She's malevolent and she hated him. That's all."

"You didn't smell burnt powder on her hands or anything like that."

"No no. Nothing."

"Well." Wolfe turned. "What about you, Mrs. Dunn? You went to pick raspberries, didn't you?"

"Yes."

"About what time?"

"Shortly after Noel went with the gun and my husband went to chop wood. We finished tea and scattered. Who told you I went to pick raspberries?"

"Your sister May. Wild raspberries?"

"No, we have a patch in a corner of the vegetable garden."

"Did you hear the shots that killed crows?"

"Yes, I did. And I heard the third shot, the—the last one. Faintly, but I heard it. Of course I thought it was only my brother still trying to get the hawk, but I'm nervous about guns and I don't like the sound no matter what is being shot. The third shot was a little before five o'clock. I quit picking raspberries and went to the arbor for some grape leaves, and when I got to the house it was ten after five."

"I understand that Titus Ames corroborates that— the time of the third shot."

June nodded. "He was in the barn milking."

"Yes. There seems to have been a great variety of activity around there. Now, Mrs. Dunn, if I asked you a lot of questions would it do me any good?"

"I don't know. I'm certainly willing to answer them."

"Do you know of anything that would help me?"

"No. I know a great many things about my brother, his character and personality, and his relations with us and other people, but nothing that I think would help you find his murderer."

"We'll have to talk it over. Not now; I'll see the others first—By the way, Mr. Dunn, I want to send a man up to your place in the country. May I have a note to Titus Ames, telling him to let my man look around, and to answer questions if he asks any? The name is Fred Durkin."

"I'll write it," June offered. "And I'll send—whom shall I send first, Mr. Wolfe?"

I put in an oar. "Your daughter, Mrs. Dunn, if you please."

"My daughter?" She looked at me in surprise. "She wasn't there. She didn't arrive until afterwards."

"We'll take her first," I said firmly.

She accepted it and crossed to her husband, and they left the room together, with his arm around her shoulders and her hand patting him on the back.

When the door had closed Wolfe asked, "Why the daughter?"

Rummaging through the desk drawers for something to take notes on, I told him, "By request. She's trying to win a prize and wants to take your picture."

Chapter 8

Sara Dunn came in on a lope, but she had to sit and wait a while until some chores were disposed of. A phone call to Saul Panzer to tell him to report to us there as soon as possible, one to Fred Durkin ditto, and one to Johnny Keems also ditto. One to Fritz to tell him we wouldn't be home for lunch. A demand, relayed by a maid to the butler, for beer. And time out for my report to Wolfe, more in detail, on the episode of Mr. Eugene Davis. After that, Wolfe sat with his lips pushing in and out for some moments, and then leaned back, sighed, and addressed the first victim.

"You told Mr. Goodwin you wanted to see me, Miss Dunn?"

"Yes," she said. It was astonishing how much her eyes were like her mother's, while her mouth and chin weren't Hawthorne at all. "I want to tell you something."

"Go ahead."

"Well . . . I suppose you know that in my parents' opinion I'm no good for anything."

"We didn't get around to discussing that point. Do you agree with them?"

"I haven't made up my mind. The trouble with me is that I'm the daughter of one of the Hawthorne girls. If they had had a lot of daughters, I suppose it would have been different, but there's only one, and I'm it. I was sick of it by the time I was ten years old, and I had an inferiority complex about the size of the perisphere. It was awful. At college they kept looking at me as if they expected suns and stars to begin shooting out of my ears. So I revolted. I ran away from college and from home too, and got a job and made enough to live on. But because I was a daughter of a Hawthorne girl I had to figure out an inexpensive way of being eccentric and audacious, and the best I could do was get a secondhand camera and take pictures of people when I wasn't supposed to. I still do it. Isn't it pathetic? You see, I have no imagination. I think up plenty of dashing things to do, but they're all either dumb or impossible or plain silly. I have no confidence in myself, not really. The glib way I'm talking to you now, that's just bluff. Inside of myself I'm trembling like a coward."

"There's nothing to tremble about." Wolfe put down his beer glass and wiped his lips with his handkerchief. "You say you ran away from home?"

She nodded. "Over a year ago. I told my mother—oh, that doesn't matter. Anyway, I severed connections, you know? I was going to carve out a canyon that would make the Hawthorne girls look like turtles in a ditch. So I got a job at twenty dollars a week selling antique glassware in a Madison Avenue shop, and bought a camera. Pretty good, no? On going

home, even for a weekend visit, I was adamant. The
first time I came close to weakening on that was last
Monday, when mother came into the shop to ask me to
come to her silver wedding anniversary. I had already
refused, in a letter. Next morning, Tuesday, Mr.
Prescott came to the shop and tried to persuade me. I
still refused, but when I quit work at six o'clock he
was in front waiting for me, with his car. I tried to
carry it off, but he carried me off instead. And, then,
when we got there, we found—Uncle Noel was dead."

Wolfe said patiently, "That was too bad. A sad
greeting for your first visit home in a year. I'm afraid
there's nothing I can do about it. Was that what you
wanted?"

"No." She was keeping her eyes aimed straight at
his. There was nothing disconcerting about them, as
there was about Naomi Karn's, but their fierce steadi-
ness gave the impression of a thrust rather than a
stare. "No," she said, "I told you that only because you
need to know it if you're going to help me. I was going
to see District Attorney Skinner this morning, but I
thought it over and realized I couldn't do it without
help. It has to be done in a way to convince him, and
everybody else, that it was I who told Uncle Noel
about that Argentina loan, and I who shot Uncle Noel
Tuesday afternoon."

My penpoint caught and spattered ink on the
paper. Wolfe demanded, "What? Say that again."

"You heard it," said Sara composedly. "One
evening—I think it was in April—I heard my father
talking about the loan with the Argentine ambassador,
and I told Uncle Noel about it to get money from him.
Recently Uncle Noel threatened to expose me—to tell

my father how he learned about the loan—and that
was why I killed him."

"I see. And since you did in fact kill him, since his
lips are sealed forever, why do you now confess these
crimes? Because your conscience bothers you?"

"No. My conscience doesn't bother me at all. I do it
to save my father from disgrace. And my mother too,
since she will share it. At the time of committing the
crimes I didn't stop to realize what the consequences
would be."

"You should have," said Wolfe gravely. "And you
should stop now to realize the consequences of your
confession. They'd trip you up in two minutes. One
thing alone; will your arm reach from Madison Avenue
to Rockland County to pull the trigger of a shotgun?
What was the phrase you used a while ago? 'Dumb or
impossible or plain silly.' You've run the gamut this
time. Think up something else. Great hounds and
Cerberus!"

"But if you'll only help me, we can do it, really we
can! I can say I left the shop—"

"Pfui! Miss Dunn, please! I'm doing a job for your
father. If you will kindly ask Miss April Hawthorne to
come here?"

It took him ten minutes to persuade her out of the
room, and at one point I was about to pick her up and
carry her. But finally she went.

Wolfe poured beer and muttered, "If they're all
like that . . ."

"You're not through with her," I told him cheerfully. "Don't forget Skinner and Cramer are downstairs. Five gets you ten she's in jail before the day's

out, and you'll have to spring her. She's our client. We sure picked a bunch of pips this time."

Before the day was out I wouldn't have minded a nice quiet cell myself, to give me a chance to think about things.

When April came in, it seemed she had a headache. She also had a retinue, sticking alongside like outriders for a royal coach, consisting of Celia Fleet, who looked as if she hadn't slept much, and Osric Stauffer, Ossie to Naomi Karn, who had been home at least long enough to change his clothes. They took chairs flanking royalty without any invitation from us.

April said, with the ripple in her voice much more subdued than it had been the day before, "I can't talk about it, I simply can't. I came because my sister said I must, but I can't talk because my throat fills up. Why should I be like that? Other people can talk no matter what happens. Something has happened to my throat."

Celia Fleet smiled at her. Stauffer gazed at her with a sickening smirk. Maybe I did the same. When she came in and pressed her hands to her temples like the heroine at the end of the second act, I had decided that the wedding was off, but it wasn't as easy as that. Something that went out from her made you forget she was a professional who knew how to get a million people to pay four-forty at the box office to watch her work. I would have died for her on the spot if I hadn't been busy taking notes.

"I doubt if you'll need to do a lot of talking," said Wolfe. "As a matter of fact, this is probably quite useless, but I have to poke around somewhere. It isn't about the will, you know. Did your sister tell you that

Mr. Dunn has engaged me to find out who killed Noel Hawthorne?"

Stauffer answered for her. "Yes," he said shortly. "And I hope to heaven you succeed. But it won't do any good to torment Miss Hawthorne about it. Last night that damned police inspector—"

"I know," Wolfe agreed. "Mr. Cramer is so forthright. I certainly don't want to torment anybody. I may not have to ask Miss Hawthorne to say anything at all. You, Miss Fleet, you were writing letters Tuesday afternoon?"

Celia nodded. "Miss Hawthorne has thousands of letters. I answer all I can. When we finished tea, about a quarter past four, I went to an alcove of the living room and was there alone, writing for about an hour, until Andy—Mr. Dunn came."

"Let's say Andy. There was another Mr. Dunn around. What did you do then?"

"Andy suggested a walk. We walked—we went to the woods—"

Celia appeared to have struck a snag. April said, "They're in love. It's a family row. Celia and I want Andy to go on the stage, he was born for it. June and her husband want him to be a lawyer and politician and get elected president. My brother wanted him in the Cullen office—my brother always wanted a son and didn't have one. We fought about it at tea. They're idiots. Andy is a rotten lawyer."

"We were in the woods a while," said Celia, "and then we went on through and came out at the other side. We didn't see anything until we stumbled on it. I nearly fell and Andy caught me—"

"I don't need all that," Wolfe interrupted. "The

chief thing is, you were writing letters at five o'clock."
He looked at April. "And you were upstairs taking a
nap."

"Yes. Mr. Stauffer asked me to go for a swim, but
I didn't feel like it. The pond's dirty."

"So you went for a swim alone." Wolfe told
Stauffer.

"Yes. The pond is in the opposite direction from the
woods, down at the foot of the hill."

Wolfe chuckled. "The police wanted to know about
that, I'll wager. Don't resent it. They're probably
making discreet inquiries right now about the opening
in Daniel Cullen and Company that Hawthorne's death
makes for you. Will you be made head of the foreign
department? Will you be made a partner? Quite a
plum—Oh, I'm not asking, but they probably are."

Stauffer had stiffened. "This is really—"

"Don't, Mr. Stauffer. What do you expect them to
do when they're after a murderer? You people are
lucky. On account of your position and standing. Even
if you killed Hawthorne yourself, you probably won't
hear a single impolite word until the district attorney
gets you on the witness stand. You might as well
escort Miss Hawthorne back to her room. I'm through
with you too, Miss Fleet. If I need—Come in!"

The door opened to admit the butler. He was
beginning to look as if he wouldn't mind going back to
his ancestral halls for a little vacation.

"Two men to see you, sir, a Mr. Panzer and a Mr.
Keems."

Wolfe told him to show them up.

Chapter 9

I laid my pen down and looked at Wolfe in extreme disgust.

"By Jiminy," I said, with the whine that I knew set his teeth on edge, "you sure are grilling them. Talk about ruthless. It gives me nervous prostration just to see them suffer. And squirm under your merciless thrusts. Lovin' babe! I don't think I ever saw you in better form—"

"Archie! Shut up!"

"But who the hell do you think you are, the inquiring reporter?"

"I do not, and I don't need that. I'm trying to think. I'm trying to think about these people, and in the meantime having another look at them. There's too many of them. If one of them sneaked through those woods and borrowed the shotgun from Noel Hawthorne and blew his head off, who is going to prove it and how?—Good afternoon, Saul. Good afternoon, Johnny. Come in. Sit down.—Am I a confounded Indian, to go up there and crawl around on my hands and knees, smelling footprints? And do you suppose any of this tribe is going to tell us anything?" He snorted. "Trying to get me interested in a family row about Andy being an actor! Bah!" He shook a finger at me menacingly. "You let me alone! One more whine out of you and—how the devil can I think if there's nothing to think about?"

I elevated my shoulders and turned my palms up. "Then we might as well go home and look at the atlas."

"I agree with you."

He abandoned me. "Did Orrie find you, Saul?"

"Yes, sir." Saul always pretended he didn't hear Wolfe and me jawing. "Miss Karn hadn't appeared when Orrie relieved me at 9:20. At 9:25 I tested her phone and she was in her apartment."

"You told Orrie to report here?"

"Yes, sir."

"You need sleep."

"I'll manage till tonight."

"You're free, are you, Johnny?"

"Yes, sir, I'm always free when you need me."

His bright eager tones, like little Willie offering to clean the blackboard, always gave me a pain. Johnny Keems was the kind of guy who does exercises every morning and buys gum at every slot vendor he sees for an excuse to look in the mirror. Dozens of times I would have resigned my job if I hadn't known his tongue was hanging out for it.

"Put this down," said Wolfe. "Both of you. Dunwoodie, Prescott & Davis, law firm on lower Broadway. Mr. Glenn Prescott. Mr. Eugene Davis. Naomi Karn got a job there as a stenographer in 1934, and after two years became the secretary of Mr. Davis. A year or so later she left to associate herself with

Mr. Noel Hawthorne in a private capacity. This is a fishing trip; I want anything you can get. Saul will direct; Johnny, you will consult with him as usual. One detail: the name of the person who did confidential stenographic work for Mr. Prescott on March 7th, 1938. If any approach is made to that person it must be with great circumspection. Johnny will of course canvass the young women with that beauty treatment outfit—what is it, Archie?"

"Nothing." I had only made a noise. The rhinoceros had the idiotic idea that when Johnny looked at a girl and smiled she melted like ice cream in the summer sun. The fact is—oh, what's the difference. He'll marry a pickpocket's daughter for her money.

They asked some questions, especially Saul, and got answers. After they had gone Wolfe went into a trance. I overlooked it and didn't try any prodding, because it was one o'clock and I knew what he was expecting. Pretty soon it arrived. The butler himself brought one tray and a maid in uniform with a split in the nail of her right index finger followed him with the other one. I saw the split when she nearly stuck the finger in my milk. Her intention was to stay and arrange things for us, but Wolfe sent her away.

He lifted the covers from the servers with a sanguine hope and a stern misgiving fighting for the mastery in his expression. When no steam came out he looked so disconcerted I could have wept. He bent over the server and glared into it incredulously.

"This is dandy," I asserted, rubbing my hands with pleasure. "Jellied consommé and a good big Waldorf salad and iced tea and these cute little wafer things—"

"Good God," he muttered, stupefied.

It was from purely selfish motives that I went downstairs myself and found somebody and requisitioned a pair of lamb chops and a pot of coffee.

The trays were empty, and Wolfe was sipping the last of the coffee, which I admit wasn't hot enough, in gloomy dissatisfaction, when the door opened and Inspector Cramer entered.

"How-do-you-do, sir," Wolfe snapped. "I'm busy."

"So I hear." Cramer crossed to a chair and sat down, got out a cigar and stuck it in his mouth and took it out again. His big phiz was redder even than usual, from the heat.

He observed, as if passing the time of day, "I understand you're working for Mr. Dunn."

Wolfe grunted offensively.

"He had a rotten lunch," I explained.

Cramer nodded. "So did I. At a drugstore counter." He surveyed Wolfe. "You look about the way I feel. I hate these damn high-life mix-ups. The lousy politicians. Every time you turn around you see a stop sign. I've got a message for you from the commissioner."

Wolfe just grunted again.

Cramer put his cigar between his teeth and said, "Maybe you've heard of him, Police Commissioner Hombert. He wants you to understand that there's to be no publicity on this thing until he says so. He also says that you're so intelligent it will be easy for you to appreciate the necessity for a lot of discretion in a case like this, involving the people it does, and that naturally you'll co-operate with me. For instance, if you were to tell me what that mob was doing in your office yesterday, we'd call that co-operation."

"Ask them," Wolfe suggested.

"I have. They're pretty remarkable. Most of them seem to be nearly as eccentric as you are. Except Mrs. Dunn, she's fairly levelheaded, and Prescott the lawyer. Prescott told me about the will. They say they went to ask you to take it up with Miss Karn and come to an understanding with her. Since when have you been a board of arbitration?"

Wolfe muttered, "Go ahead. Come to the point."

"I will. Is that what they went to your office for? To get you to make a deal with Miss Karn?"

"Yes."

"But you had Miss Karn right there, didn't you? By the way, you might have told me who she was when I asked you, but I suppose that would be too much to expect. Anyway, these people have all got tongues in their heads, and they had their lawyer along. What was it they wanted you to do that they couldn't do themselves?"

Wolfe shrugged. "They had been informed that I am able, astute, discreet and unscrupulous."

"Hell, I could have told them that." Cramer removed his cigar from his mouth and studied the tip of it. "I've been trying to figure out what they needed you for when they already had a good lawyer. I like things to be plausible. What if they suspected Miss Karn had murdered Hawthorne, and they wanted you to sort of collect evidence and put it in shape? That would be a good job for a detective. Then Miss Karn could sign an agreement to let them have the dough, or most of it, and you could decide the evidence wasn't good enough to justify accusing her of murder. So everybody would be satisfied, except maybe Hawthorne, but he was dead. How do you like that way of figuring it?"

"I think it's clumsy," said Wolfe judiciously. "If they regarded me as capable of compromising with a murderer, they would also have thought it likely that I would retain the evidence and blackmail them the rest of their lives. Not to mention the detail that they weren't aware Hawthorne had been murdered. You saw their shock and surprise when you told them he had."

"Yeah, I saw that. They certainly were shocked."

"Indeed they were." Wolfe frowned. "Then aren't you supporting the theory that Hawthorne was killed because he had ruined Mr. Dunn's career with that Argentina loan business? I thought you fellows had that all cooked and ready to serve."

"I'm not a cook, I'm a cop. If anybody uses this murder to grease someone's pants, it won't be me. I'm supposed to be looking for a murderer. From what Dunn tells me, so are you."

"I am."

"Okay. Let's find him or her. I'm going to be frank with you. I like the idea of Miss Karn. Personally. You don't need to tell Skinner that. She inherits seven million dollars, and there have been plenty of murders for a hell of a lot less than that. Since she was intimate with Hawthorne, of course she knew where he was going that day and who would be there. She drives a car. She went there to get him, probably with a gun. She went there to do it because she knew there were a dozen people there who would be good suspects for one reason or another. She had a piece of luck and saw him from the road, there by the edge of the woods, with a shotgun. She walked across the field and chinned with him, maneuvered him around to the corner of the woods that can't be seen from the road, .made some excuse to get hold of the shotgun, and killed him. She didn't even have to use her own weapon. Then she wiped the shotgun with a bunch of grass, put his prints on it, and beat it."

Wolfe grumbled, "Anyone of a million people could have done all that."

"Uh-huh. But it only took one to do it. I'm enthusiastic about the idea of Miss Karn, especially after the talk I had with her this morning. Of course I'm not subtle like you, but I know a two-legged female tiger when I see one. She's a dangerous baby, that Karn woman is. It's in her eyes. Incidentally, you can have this for nothing, she has no alibi for Tuesday afternoon. She thinks she has, but that kind is two for a nickel."

The inspector lowered his chin and elevated his cigar. "Now just suppose. Andy Dunn and the Fleet girl, and Dunn himself and that Stauffer, were the first ones at the scene when the body was found. Suppose they looked around out of curiosity and one of them found something. A lady's compact or a pack of cigarettes or a handkerchief—anything. Maybe they knew it belonged to Miss Karn and maybe not. Maybe Stauffer did—he knows her. Maybe they just decided to ditch it on general principles, thinking no lady should be involved. Then they got a sock in the eye when the will was read. The whole pile, except a measly half million, to Miss Karn! So they put their heads together, and if you ask me, Prescott was in it too. But it was too ticklish for him to handle it himself.

They went to you and showed you the compact or whatever it was. Maybe they already knew it belonged to Miss Karn, or maybe it was part of your job to prove that. Anyhow you were to put the screws on her.

"And now that the murder's out, where are they and where are you? They can't open the bag even if they wanted to, without admitting that they concealed knowledge of a crime and evidence of it. And they wouldn't want to even if they could, because if she was tried and convicted the estate would be divided by the court, and if she was tried and acquitted it would all be hers and they could whistle. Don't you think that's logical?"

Wolfe nodded. "Perfect," he declared. "I congratulate you. I don't see a loophole in it anywhere. Did you suppose all that without any help?"

"I did. For help I'm coming to you. Here I am and there it is. I'm making you a proposition. Cough it up, and get them to do the same, and I guarantee no trouble and no publicity on that angle of it for anybody concerned. I guarantee to handle Skinner. I realize you'll have to consult them first, and I'll give you until nine o'clock tomorrow morning."

Wolfe said in a silky voice, "It's regrettable. Nearly every order you place with me is something I haven't in stock. Good day, sir, Archie—"

"Wait a minute." Cramer's eyes had narrowed. "This time you're going to lose. This time, thank God, I've got more than you to work on. I can crack one or more of that outfit wide open, and I'm going to. Then you know where you'll be. I've come to you with an absolutely fair offer—"

"You've charged me," Wolfe snapped, "with being a knave and a nincompoop. Good day, sir."

"I'll give you until—"

"Don't give me anything. I don't want it."

"You're a damn bullheaded boob."

Inspector Cramer got up and walked out of the room. Wolfe winced when the door slammed.

"It's a funny thing and a sad thing," I observed, "that the purer our motives are, the worse insults we get. Do you remember the time—"

"That will do, Archie. Get Mrs. Hawthorne."

I groaned. "I don't want her."

"I do. Get her."

I departed. In the hall I met the maid coming to get our trays, and she informed me that Mrs. Hawthorne's apartments were on the floor above, so I sought the stairs and mounted another flight. I knocked on the right door if the maid knew what she was talking about, the third time good and loud, but with no result. Ordinarily I would have opened the door for a look, but I didn't like the errand I was on anyway, so I moved on to the next one and tried that. No go. I ventured across the hall and tapped on another one, beyond which there seemed to be faint hum of voices, received an invitation to come in, pushed it open and entered.

I had interrupted a conference. They stopped it to look at me. Andy Dunn and Celia Fleet were side by side on a sofa, holding hands, and seated next to them was May Hawthorne, in a faded old blue house gown, with her hair making for her right eye. I'd hate to say what she looked like. Standing in front of them was Glenn Prescott, spruce and cool-looking in a white linen suit with a yellow flower in his buttonhole that was no dianthus superbus, but beyond that I wouldn't say. On a chair at his right was Daisy Hawthorne, in the same gray outfit, including veil, she had worn for her now-you-see-me-now-you-don't in the living room that morning.

I bowed gracefully. "Excuse me, Mrs. Hawthorne. Mr. Wolfe asks if you will kindly come to the library."

Prescott frowned. "I would like to have a talk with Mr. Wolfe myself. Mr. Dunn tells me he has engaged him—"

"Yes, sir. I'll tell him you're here. Right now he wants to see Mrs. Hawthorne—If you please?"

She got up and moved.

"Very well," Prescott conceded. "I'll be here or below in the music room with Mr. Dunn."

I opened the door for Daisy to precede me, and followed her downstairs and let her into the library. Wolfe, greeting her, made his customary excuse for failing to arise as she crossed to the chair Cramer had vacated. She said, in her high-pitched voice with a distortion too faint to be called an impediment of speech:

"I don't know what you expect to learn from me. Do you think I can tell you anything?"

"No, Mrs. Hawthorne, I don't," Wolfe told her politely. "I doubt if anyone here is going to tell me anything. I'm just shuffling around in the dark with my hand in front of my face. If you will tell me briefly—" He frowned, turning. "Come in!"

It was the butler. "A man to see you, sir. Durkin."

"Please send him up at once."

I expected this to be diverting enough to take my

mind off the veil, for more than three hours had passed since I had phoned Fred to come to 67th Street at once. But as it turned out, the diversion came from another quarter. Fred started talking loud and fast as he came through the door:

"The reason I'm late, Mr. Wolfe, after Archie phoned I thought I'd just lie there a minute and get things straight in my mind, and after the night I've had I wouldn't have been much good anyway, and now I'm—"

"You went to sleep again," said Wolfe ominously.

"Yes, sir, and the missus should of woke me but she didn't. Anyhow, now my head's on my shoulders and I'm strung like a lyre. As I just told Orrie, I can do more—"

"Who told who?"

"Orrie Cather. I told him I can—"

"Where did you see Orrie?"

"Down at the corner just now. I—"

"What corner?"

"Out front. Across the street. I told him—"

"Be quiet." Wolfe looked at me and snapped, "Go and find out."

I hopped for the hall, trotted downstairs and on out to the street, crossed to the other side, and turned left. He was there at the exit of an areaway. As I passed I gave him a sign, and then went on and turned the corner. I waited, and he joined me.

"What do you mean," I demanded, "chinning with Fred when you're solo?"

"Chin yourself," he retorted. "I wasn't chinning, he was. I chased him."

"And what are you doing here? Got a date with a governess?"

"No, Colonel, I'm working. You baboon, what do you think I'm doing? She's in there."

"Where?"

"The house you came out of."

"I'll be damned. How long ago?"

"We arrived at 2:28. Twenty-seven minutes ago."

"I am damned. Okay, sit on it."

I trotted back the way I had come, pushed the button and was admitted by the butler. I stopped in the entrance hall to consider things, and he stood and looked at me until I waved him away. The point was that knowing Wolfe as I did, I was aware that if I went up to him and reported that Naomi Karn was somewhere in the house, he would immediately ask, "Where?" So I called the butler back and inquired, "Could you tell me where Miss Karn is? The lady who arrived about half an hour ago."

"Yes, sir. She is in the living room with Mrs. Hawthorne."

It sounded goofy to me. I decided that eyesight was better than hearsay, made for the wide doorway to the living room, and went on through; and saw at a glance that sight was just as goofy as sound. On one of the chairs toward the far end was Naomi Karn, in the same blue linen thing she had worn to Wolfe's the day before, and on another one, directly facing her, was Daisy Hawthorne. They both looked at me, at least Naomi did, and the veil turned my way.

I said, "Excuse me," and beat it for the hall and the stairs. There would be nothing to tell Wolfe, since of course it was in his presence that Daisy had been informed of the caller who had arrived.

But, opening the library door and entering, I saw that was wrong. There certainly was something to tell him. He was talking to Fred, who stood twisting his hat and looking uncomfortable, and Daisy Hawthorne was sitting there in her chair.

Chapter 10

Evidently I lost my aplomb. I may even have
stared with my jaw hanging open. Anyhow, I
came to when Wolfe fired at me:

"What's the matter with you? Palsy?"

Fred Durkin says I tittered. I did not. I merely
said in a composed tone, "Mr. Brenner would like to
speak to you a moment privately. In the hall."

He glared at me suspiciously, then lifted his bulk
with a grunt, crossed, and passed through the door
which I opened. I pulled the door shut.

"Well?" he demanded.

I said in an undertone, "We're being stalked.
Engage in earnest whispered conversation, mumble
umble, diddie riggie . . ."

The footsteps I had heard became Mr. John
Charles Dunn and his wife June. Coming up the stairs,
they reached our level, and, turning for the corridor,
saw us. Dunn called:

"Have you seen Prescott, Mr. Wolfe? He's here and
wants to talk with you."

Wolfe replied that he hadn't seen the lawyer but

would do so presently. Dunn nodded and, his wife beside him, dragged his feet along the corridor to the next flight of stairs. As soon as they were out of sight I switched to English again:

"Naomi Karn is down in the living room, but that's not what gave me palsy. Daisy Hawthorne is there with her, talking to her."

He growled, "What the devil did you drag me out here for? If you think this is a time for childish flummery—"

"No, sir, I don't. Far from it. I'm telling you, the veiled widow is there in the library. She is also downstairs chatting with Naomi Karn. I just this second saw her. Someone's playing a funny joke. But who's the joke on, us up here, or Naomi down there?"

"Do you mean to tell me someone is masquerading—"

"Yeah, that's the idea. These Hawthorne girls certainly are cards. But which is which?"

"In the living room talking with Miss Karn?"

"Yep."

"You just saw them?"

"Yep."

"Did you see Orrie?"

"Yep. She led him here at 2:28 and was admitted by the butler."

He frowned at me a moment, pursing his lips, and then said, "Ask Fred to come here."

I did so. Wolfe told him: "Go on up there and do your utmost to keep awake. Don't lose the letter to Mr. Ames. Don't get in a fight. I'll be either here or at home."

"Mr. Wolfe, I'm sorry I—"

"So am I. Go on."

Fred went. Wolfe eyed me. "Now. We don't need to flounder around with this. I'll sit where I was. You sit beyond her. I'll ask you to hand me something, and as you pass her you will lift that confounded veil."

"I don't want to."

"I don't blame you. Please open the door."

That was one of the times I would have resigned on the spot but for the practical certainty that he would have given the job to Johnny Keems out of pure cussedness. I am not a softy. I once smacked a dainty little Cuban lassie out of her senses when she came to the office with a dagger in her sock, with the intention of presenting it to Nero Wolfe point first because he had draped a smuggling job around the neck of her black-eyed boy friend. But as I followed Wolfe back into the library and obeyed his instructions by taking a chair the other side of our version of Daisy Hawthorne, I was gulping down repugnance till I could feel it sticking in my throat.

However, I did it. I mean I tried to. First Wolfe asked a few questions and got her to talk a little. As near as I could tell, her voice, high-pitched, with a strain in it that gave you the feeling that it wasn't coming from a mouth, was exactly the same as it had been in the office the day before. I decided it was either Daisy herself or the best mimic I had ever heard; and it was in my mind, naturally, that while a great actress isn't necessarily a fine mimic, by public repute April Hawthorne was. Wolfe tried another trick, asking her what time it was, but when she looked at her wrist watch she did so with exactly the same slant to her head, using the left eye apparently, as the previous day when she had read the paper he gave her.

Wolfe asked me to hand him the notes I had taken of the interview with the others. I got up and started for him. When I was even with her chair I stumbled and lurched against her and grabbed to keep from falling, and what I got hold of was the lower edge of the veil. I knew it was anchored and would take a good jerk, and since it had to be done I was going to do it right, but I simply wasn't prepared for what happened. A hurricane hit me. An awful screech split the air, and thirty wildcats flew at my face, which wasn't protected by any veil, with all their claws working. Being stubborn, I was going on through and die fighting, but Wolfe called my name sharply and I jammed on the brake. She was ten feet away, and I never have been able to figure out how she got there and performed mayhem simultaneously.

"You clumsy fool," said Wolfe. "Apologize."

"Yes, sir." I looked at the veil, as intact as if I'd never touched it. "I stumbled. I'm very sorry, Mrs. Hawthorne."

"The door," said Wolfe. "That scream must have alarmed people."

As I reached it I heard hurried footsteps outside, and, opening it, saw Andy Dunn and his father looking white and startled, trotting toward me, and in the background Celia Fleet's white shirt and blouse and the faded blue gown May Hawthorne was sporting. I sang out, "Okay! Sorry! I slipped and fell and scared Mrs. Hawthorne! Excuse it please!"

They said something which I shut off by closing the door almost in their faces. Apparently my explanation

satisfied them that we hadn't bumped Daisy off and
the scream wasn't her expiring cry, for they didn't
enter to investigate. I looked around for a mirror and
didn't see one. My face felt as if someone had scattered
gunpowder on it and touched a match.

"You'd better find a bathroom and wash that blood
off," said Wolfe curtly. "Then please go down to the
living room and get the notes you left there. Look
them over and see if they're what I want."

I was too irate to speak, so I departed without a
word. In the bathroom down the hall I surveyed the
devastation in the mirror. My lovely smooth skin was
a sight. "Occupational hazard," I said bitterly. "To hell
with it. I'm going to get a job as an executive." I wet
a towel and dabbed at it and did it smart.

And what Wolfe had meant, of course, was that I
was to proceed to the living room, to the other Daisy,
and turn the other cheek. If he thought I was going to
represent the firm at any more unveiling ceremonies,
he was deficient above the neck, but in my judgment
that would prove unnecessary. I did not believe that
anyone, even April Hawthorne, could act the part of
thirty wildcats with that amount of fervor; that one in
the library actually was thirty wildcats. I had not
observed the other one with any particularity, and
hadn't heard her speak; probably a few sharp glances
and a little conversation would do the trick. So when I
had done all I could with the dabbing I moseyed on
downstairs to the living room.

I was too late. Naomi Karn was still there, seated
in the same chair as before, but she was alone. I
walked over to her. Her eyes slanted up at me, and I
met them. My mind was sufficiently on something else

so that as far as I was concerned she was about as dangerous as a snake charmer in a circus.

I said, "I wanted to ask Mrs. Hawthorne something. Do you know where she went?"

Miss Karn shook her head. "She said she'd be back shortly."

"How long ago did she leave?"

"How long? Oh, ten minutes."

"I just wondered, because Mr. Wolfe is expecting her upstairs, when she gets through with you." I gazed down at her. "I told Mr. Wolfe you're here, and he said it would be a shame if you closed a deal with these people yourself, since in that case we'd be out a fee."

"I'm not interested in your fee."

"No, I suppose not. Did Mrs. Hawthorne phone and ask you to come, or did you just come?"

She let that one go by. A corner of her lip curled. "You may tell Mr. Wolfe that his bluff didn't work. I have learned that his ridiculous offer of a hundred thousand dollars was not authorized by his clients. I'll do a great deal better than that."

"Good. We don't deserve a fee anyhow. I am strongly opposed to the detective tariff. Why should you contribute to our sensual ease? I agree with whoever it was, millions for defemmes but not one cent for tribute. Excuse me a minute."

A sudden bright idea had occurred to me. The draperies, heavy red folds from the ceiling to the floor, behind which Daisy had disappeared that morning, were there in the middle of the wall only three paces away. My idea was vague; there was no sense in supposing that she had chosen that exit again and was

there eavesdropping; but I was curious about what
was behind them anyhow. I stepped over and parted
them enough to look in. Then, seeing what I saw, I
passed through and let them fall behind me.

Osric Stauffer stood there, his back to the wall,
with his finger pressed against his lips to shush me. I
met his eyes, and met an appeal for silence there too,
in spite of the dim light.

I glanced around. It was a small room, with a small
window in the left rear corner. At one side was a bar,
about ten feet long, with an array of glasses and
bottles on shelves behind it, and a big picture of
barefooted girls picking grapes. A rug on the floor
completed the furnishings. In the right rear corner
was a door, shut.

Stauffer hadn't moved. He didn't look very menac-
ing, so I saw no reason to interfere with his method of
passing the time. I turned around and pawed my way
out and was standing in front of Miss Karn again.

"When Mrs. Hawthorne comes back," I said, "I'd
appreciate it if you'd finish with her as soon as
possible, because Mr. Wolfe wants her. Why don't you
come up and see Wolfe while you're waiting? He'd love
to have a chat with you."

She just looked through me. I shrugged. "Okay,
suit yourself. I understand you had a good talk with an
old friend of mine this morning. Inspector Cramer. He
was warning Wolfe about you and telling about your
alibis for Tuesday afternoon."

She stirred on her chair. "I doubt," she said, "if at
any time in my life I would have regarded you as
funny."

"Pooh." I looked her in the eye. "Let me tell you

something, Miss Karn. Up to now I am reserving judgment as to whether it was you who blew Hawthorne's head off. If it was, you'd better be making your own will instead of fussing around about his. But if it wasn't, the best thing you can do is trot upstairs without delay and lay your pretty head confidingly on Nero Wolfe's shoulder. I'm telling you. The popping noises around here do not come from firecrackers, which might singe your eyelashes but that's all. Someone's going to get a bad burn out of this before it's over."

Leaving that for her to consider at leisure, I marched off. Reflecting that if the downstairs Daisy was the counterfeit she had had plenty of time to discard her masquerade, and that therefore peeking through keyholes would have been wasted effort, I decided on a swift gallop around the field before returning to G.H.Q. The result was negative. I dispensed with such niceties as knocking on doors. The other three rooms on the ground floor, including the music room, were uninhabited. In a sitting room one flight up, two doors from the library, I flushed Dunn and his wife, and Prescott, apparently discussing their troubles. Mrs. Hawthorne's apartment on the floor above was empty. Andy Dunn and Celia Fleet saw me enter it and leave it, from a bench they were occupying in the hall. They didn't look interrupted; evidently they weren't discussing anything, just sitting close enough to touch. In the room across the hall where I had found the library edition of Daisy when Wolfe sent me after her, May Hawthorne was lying on a bed with her bare feet protruding beyond the hem of the veteran gown, and her eyes closed. She asked, "Who is it?" without moving or opening her eyes, and I said, "Nobody much," and went out again.

That left two to go. I found them together, in a room at the street end of the corridor. April was stretched out on a chaise longue, with her arms flung above her head, dressed in a green thing of thin silk which smoothed itself out on her high spots like a soft skin, and wearing no veil. Sara was on a chair near her, with a book open. Sara stared at me. April's head didn't move, but she got me from the corner of her eyes.

She said, "You might knock, you know. Does that man want me again?"

"No, I'm just looking."

"Thank heaven." She sighed with relief. "My niece is reading 'The Cherry Orchard' to me. Of course I know it by heart. Would you care to listen?"

I said no, much obliged, and departed. Having observed a writing desk in Daisy Hawthorne's suit, I returned there, found some paper in a drawer, got out my pen and sat down and wrote:

> *Downstairs Daisy disappeared. Told Naomi would return shortly but hasn't. Naomi, waiting for her return, scorns you and says I'm not funny. Stauffer is lurking behind a curtain ten feet from her, God knows why. Made a survey and everyone accounted for. Sara is reading "The Cherry Orchard" (Chekhov) to April. Either one could have done it. I resign.*

I blotted it, went out and descended to the library, and handed it to Wolfe, saying:

"I doubt if that's it. It's the only one I left in the living room."

As he read it I got myself into a chair, this time one at the end of the desk, as far as practical from our own Daisy. I glanced at her sitting there behind her screen, and then looked somewhere else.

Wolfe grunted and passed the paper back to me. "It can wait. Mrs. Hawthorne and I have been discussing the matter of the will. It is her opinion that it expresses the wishes of her husband and his deliberate intention to deprive her of her rightful share of his fortune. She is not surprised at her husband's duplicity, but strongly resents the fact that Mr. Prescott did not inform her of the will's contents at the time it was drawn, though I have told her that had he done so it would have been a flagrant breach of ethics. Please make a note of these remarks. I asked Mrs. Hawthorne if she has dealt, or attempted to deal, directly with Miss Karn in the matter, and she says she has not and would not. I believe that covers the points we've discussed, madam?"

"Yes." The veil inclined slightly forward and straightened up again.

Wolfe regarded it with half-closed eyes. "Well. Has Mr. Dunn told you that he has asked me to investigate your husband's death?"

"No, but his wife has. My sister-in-law June."

"Have you talked with the police?"

The veil was inclined again. "Last night. The district attorney. Mr. Skinner."

"Are you willing to discuss it with me? I want to say, Mrs. Hawthorne, that I realize I am in your home, this is the library of your home, and I thank you for allowing me to work here. I assure you I shall clear out at the earliest possible moment. The luncheon—I shall not impose upon you for another meal if I can help it. But I do have a few questions to ask."

"I am perfectly willing to answer them. I don't believe—I doubt if I can help your investigation any, although I know quite well who killed my husband."

"Oh. You do?"

"Yes. April."

She had a special way of saying "April." Anyone hearing her and not knowing what was meant would have guessed that April was a cross between a cockroach and a rattlesnake.

"I should think," said Wolfe, "that will help my investigation a good deal. Provided you can give any reasons."

"I can. April is sunk in debt and expected a legacy. She intends to marry Osric Stauffer. She pretends she's playing with him, but she isn't, she intends to marry him. She knows her beauty is going and she'll need him. She thinks he'll succeed to my husband's partnership in Daniel Cullen and Company. She hated Noel's influence over Andy. She wants Andy to marry that little blond fool Celia and be an actor. She knew Noel was leaving me next to nothing in his will, and she wanted me to have that blow too."

She stopped. Wolfe asked, "Is that all?"

"Yes."

"But you can't have both ends, Mrs. Hawthorne. If she knew your husband was leaving you next to nothing, she must also have known what she was to get. A peach."

"Not at all. Noel fooled them too. He told her what he was doing to me, but not what he was doing to her."

"Do you have evidence of that?"

"I don't need any." The strain in her voice was more intense. "I know what my husband was like."

"Do you possess any evidence that April Hawthorne did shoot her brother?"

"I don't possess any, no. But she did."

"You know, I suppose, that she says she was upstairs sleeping at the time it happened."

"I know," said the veil contemptuously. "But she wasn't."

"Did you see her leave the house or sneak into the woods?"

"No."

Wolfe sighed. "I was hoping perhaps you had. I understand you were out in a field picking black-eyed susans."

"I was picking daisies."

"All right, daisies. I haven't seen a map of the grounds, so I wouldn't know whether you could see the house or the border of the woods from where you were. Could you?"

"Not the house actually, on account of trees around it. Besides the woods skirting the hill, there are clumps of trees all around there. They shielded me— that is, they shielded the house from my view, and the woods too. The reason I made that slip of the tongue—I am accustomed to regard myself as being in need of shielding." A long thin finger touched the edge of the veil.

"Of course. I wouldn't call that a slip. From where you were could you hear all three of the gunshots?"

"I don't know whether I could or not, but I didn't. The first shot was when we were finishing tea on the lawn; we spoke about it. Soon after that I went to the field for daisies. I heard no more shots. Often when I am alone like that my mind is on—on myself. That may be comprehensible to you. Perhaps I could have heard the shots, but I didn't."

"I see." Wolfe closed his eyes. After a moment he opened them again and directed them at the veil. "If I were you," he suggested, "I'd be a little circumspect about stating what you know, when you possess no evidence. After this thing gets in the papers it will be pretty nasty."

"Nasty?" That awful little laugh fluttered the veil. "You mean what I said about April."

"Yes. If she committed murder she'll probably pay for it. In the meantime—"

"But she did! I know she did! I possess no evidence, but someone else does!"

"Indeed. Who?"

"I don't know."

"Where is it?"

"I don't know."

"What is it?"

"I know that, but it wouldn't do any good to tell you."

"I'll decide that," Wolfe snapped. "Did you tell Mr. Skinner about it."

"No. It wouldn't do any good to tell him either." The high-pitched voice went higher yet. "They would just deny it! How could I prove it? But I heard them, and I saw it!"

"Maybe I can prove it, Mrs. Hawthorne. I'd like to try. What was it?"

"It was a cornflower. Andy found a cornflower there near Noel's body! And April had a bunch of them stuck in her belt when we were there having tea on the lawn!"

Chapter 11

Wolfe let out a little growl and made himself more comfortable in his chair. He said nothing.

Daisy spoke again. Her voice had been shrill with excitement, but now it went flat. She muttered, "I didn't intend to tell you that."

"Why not?" Wolfe demanded.

"Because it won't do any good. I can't prove it and they'll deny it. But if I had kept it to myself . . ."

"You might have found an occasion to use it. Was that the idea?"

"Yes. Why shouldn't I?" Her voice went up the scale again, in defiance. "Even though they knew I couldn't prove it—and like a fool I blurt it out to you."

"It can't be helped now." Wolfe's tone was smooth, even sympathetic. "I doubt if you could have used it effectively, anyway. They're a pretty tough crowd. You say April had a bunch of cornflowers in her belt while you were having tea on the lawn Tuesday afternoon?"

"Yes."

"You might as well tell me about it. Maybe we can figure out a way of proving it."

"You can't. How can you? Osric Stauffer picked them in the garden and brought them and gave them to her and she stuck them in at her waist. She had on a green blouse and yellow slacks. We commented on the blue of the cornflowers with the other colors."

"Did Mr. Stauffer keep one for himself?"

"Why, I—" She considered. "No, he didn't."

"Or give some to anyone else?"

"No. He gave them all to April."

"Did she leave the gathering on the lawn before you? Or was she still there when you left?"

"She was still there. They all were except Noel and John."

Scribbling along with my pen, I allowed myself a satisfied grin. Wolfe was working at last, picking up all the pieces he could find, methodically and patiently. He spent twenty minutes with her getting the complete picture of the tea party, and another ten with her in the field, collecting black-eyed susans, daisies to her and nothing at all to me. She had returned to the house with her arms full of them, more than an hour later, and was making arrangements in vases, when Celia Fleet burst in asking for Dunn in an agitated voice. She had followed Celia, unobtrusively, and had been within earshot when Dunn received the news of what Andy had found in the briar patch beyond the woods.

"I wasn't eavesdropping," she declared, not defensively, merely imparting information. "I was later, when I heard Andy telling them about the cornflower. I actually saw it."

Wolfe inquired, "What time was that?"

"It was late that evening, about eleven o'clock. Even then I—well, I won't say I suspected that Noel had been murdered, but I knew of the feeling between him and John on account of that Argentina loan business, and other feelings there were around there, and I was curious and vaguely suspicious. So after the sheriff and doctor had gone away, I went to my room but I didn't go to bed. I noticed some of them hadn't come upstairs, and I went down without making any noise and out the back way. It was a hot night and windows were open everywhere, and there was a light from the dining room. I could hear low voices as I got closer, and then I could see them, John and June and Andy. Andy was telling them about finding the cornflower, and took it from his pocket and showed it to them. He said it had been there about fifteen feet from Noel's body, caught on a branch of a rose briar, and he had taken it and put it in his pocket. He said it hadn't occurred to him at the moment, but it had since, the idea that April had been there for a private talk with Noel and had lost it from the bunch she was wearing. But of course, he said, that wasn't how it got there, because April had stated that she had been in her room taking a nap. John said calmly that it was true the cornflower couldn't have been dropped by April, since she hadn't been there, but that Andy had been quite right to bring it away and thereby avoid the possibility of a lot of unpleasant and irrelevant questions just because a cornflower had been found hanging on a briar. They were very casual about it, but they knew better. Their tone and the way they looked—they knew. And so did I. I knew then, as I

went back up the dark stairs, that April had killed
Noel."

Wolfe wiggled a finger at her. "You knew nothing
of the sort, madam."

"But I tell you—it's no wonder you—you're on
their side—"

"Rubbish. I'm not on anybody's side; I'm hunting a
murderer. I admit the cornflower is evidence, probably extremely important evidence, but of what? Of
April's guilt? Perhaps. Or of an attempt by the murderer to incriminate April by getting a cornflower
from the garden and leaving it near the body? Perhaps. Rather inconclusive, but fairly ingenious at that.
Do you by any chance know what happened to the
cornflower?"

"No. I suppose John destroyed it. I said I couldn't
prove it. But you must believe—you must—you
signed that paper promising to safeguard my
interests—"

"Oh, I believe you all right. But my commitment in
that paper was limited to the negotiations regarding
the will. Please understand that. There is, after all, a
remote possibility that you killed your husband yourself. I should think you might measure up to that
cornflower trick."

"Now you're talking rubbish."

"Perhaps. You ought to know. How long were the
stems of the bouquet Stauffer presented to April?"

He got patient and methodical again. As I listened
to them chewing away, putting down their syllables
automatically on the unruled paper which had been
the best I could find, I reflected that this appeared to
be shaping up for a honey. The only nugget in the

pouch so far was this cornflower on a briar, and that was certainly nothing to write home about, with a garden right there full of cornflower bushes, provided they grew on bushes. Not to mention the chance that Daisy had made it all up just to keep her brain occupied. I was idly considering alternatives when the phone buzzed, and I went and got it. It was Saul Panzer. By the time I got through taking his concise but detailed report, Wolfe had finished with Daisy and she was arising to leave.

I opened to door to let her out, and returned to the desk.

"If you ask me," I remarked, "we would have been a hell of a sight better off if we had stuck to the last will and testament and let the murder go. Of all the—"

"That was Saul?"

"Yes, sir."

"Well?"

"He has been conferring with elevator operators and bootblacks et al. Johnny got orders for five beauty outfits before he was tossed out on his ear, and he had a date to buy a lady a dinner at the Polish Pavilion this evening. That will cost you dear. Davis is married and lives with his wife, at least nominally. He and Naomi had a romance when she was his secretary. The sort of thing May Hawthorne comprehends intellectually. L'amour. He has gone moody and taken to drink. So far information very sketchy; nothing particular on Prescott yet, except that he gives people expensive cigars, pays good salaries, and is not a knee-toucher. Saul has lines out that are promising. No start on Prescott's confidential stenographer in March, 1938."

Wolfe had his lips compressed. "I hate to waste

Saul—" He shrugged. "It can't be helped. What time is it?"

"Five after five. Would you care to go into the matter of the duplicate Daisy?"

"Not now. Mr. Prescott wants to see me. First some beer. Then see if Miss Karn is still down there, and who is with her. Then Mr. Prescott."

I trotted out and descended to the main floor. There was no one around the entrance hall, so I opened a door leading to the rear of the house and yelled, "Turner!" In a moment a maid appeared and said he was upstairs, and I said all I wanted was to order three bottles of beer for Mr. Wolfe in the library. Then I proceeded to the living room for a glimpse of Naomi Karn.

But I didn't get it. She was absent. The only person in the room was a man of about my build, pacing up and down with his fists making his pockets bulge. I stopped short and regarded him with surprise. He had put his pants on, but I recognized him anyway.

I said, "Hello."

He quit pacing and scowled at me. Before he said a word I knew exactly the condition he was in, more from observation than from personal experience. You drink all night, and pass out, and someone takes you home and drops you on a bed. When you come to, there is no telling what day it is or when they started running the subway inside your head or how many people came to your funeral. But something drastic must be done immediately. You get your pants and shoes on and fight your way to the street and along to and into a place, order a double Scotch and gulp it

down, spilling maybe a quarter of it. You spill much
less of the second one, and by the time the third one
comes along you have nearly stopped trembling and
you don't waste a drop. Then, while you still are not
quite ready to tell the date on a calendar, you have a
strong impression that you are prepared to cope with
whatever it is that requires coping, and off you go.

"Who are you?" he demanded, in a voice that made
me afraid he would strip his gears. "I want Glenn
Prescott."

"Yes, sir," I said ingratiatingly. "I know you do. If
you will come this way, please."

"I'm not coming that way or any other way." He
planted himself. His fists were still bulging in his
pockets. "He can come here. You can go and tell
him—"

"Yes, sir, I will. But this is a sort of a public room.
People come in here all the time. These chairs are no
good to sit on, either. I'll be glad to bring Mr. Prescott
wherever you say, but I do honestly think the library
would be much better." I backed toward the doorway.
"Come and see for yourself. If you don't like it you can
return here."

"I'll like it all right, but he won't." He stayed
planted. Then abruptly he rumbled, "You don't need to
show me the library, I know where it is," and moved
so fast he nearly toppled me over as he went by.

I was at his heels going up the stairs, and stayed
there, thinking to steer him in case he was too
optimistic about knowing where the library was, but
he went straight to the door and flung it open. I
followed him in, closed the door, and announced to
Wolfe:

"Mr. Eugene Davis."

Davis glared around. "Where's Prescott?" He glared at Wolfe. "Who are you?" He glared at me. "What kind of a run-around is this? You're not Turner! I sent Turner to get Prescott!"

"That's all right," I said soothingly, "we'll get him. I'm not a butler, I'm a detective. Detectives are better than butlers for getting people. This is Mr. Nero Wolfe."

"Who the hell—"

He stopped abruptly. You might have thought I had reached inside his skull and flipped a switch. A sort of spasm went over his face, and his shoulders stiffened and then relaxed again, and when he focused his eyes on Wolfe they were no longer merely bleary and foolishly truculent. They were alert and intelligent and on guard.

"Oh," he said. His tone had changed even more than his eyes. "You're Nero Wolfe."

Wolfe nodded. "Yes, sir."

"You're here helping to prove Hawthorne was murdered. Or that he wasn't. I see." He turned to survey me. "So Turner announced me to you instead of to Prescott. And told you I was drunk, I suppose. It's Prescott I came here to see. I'll find him."

He started off, but Wolfe snapped, "One minute, Mr. Dawson!"

Halfway to the door, he halted, stood there for four seconds with his back to us, and then slowly turned around. "My name's Davis," he said with careful precision. "Eugene Davis."

"Not on 11th Street. There it's Earl Dawson. And how did you know Hawthorne was murdered? Did Mr.

Prescott tell you? Or did you learn it from Miss Karn
when you were dining with her last evening?"

He had things under control all right. Knowing the
feeling he must have been experiencing in his stomach
under the circumstances, I admired him. All he did
was stand and gaze at Wolfe and chew his lower lip.
Finally he crossed to a chair, steadily and without
haste, sat down, and asked:

"What do you want?"

"I want to talk with you, Mr. Davis."

"What about?"

"This mess. This murder. This will business."

"I know nothing about either one. How did you
know I am Earl Dawson on 11th Street?"

"You drank to excess last night. A man who works
for me took you home and removed your trousers.
Another man who works for me—Mr. Goodwin here,
Mr. Archie Goodwin—went there this morning and
identified you from articles in your pockets. As for
your dining with Miss Karn, she was being followed."

"Of course. I should have thought of that. I was
stupid. It still surprises me to realize I was stupid,
because originally I wasn't meant to be. About my
being Dawson, I would like to know who has been
informed. The police?"

"No. No one. Mr. and Mrs. Dunn know that you
were found somewhere in a drunken stupor, but not
where, and not that you were incognito."

"Is that straight?"

"Yes, sir. I would have no compunction about lying
to you, but that's straight."

"I'll take it that way." I could see that the finger-
nails of his right hand were digging into his palm. He

saw that I saw it, and stuck the hand into his coat pocket. He went on, "In view of the way things are, I suppose it's an affectation for me to try to keep the Dawson thing—that place—secret, but as I say, I can't be counted on any more not to act stupidly. I don't want that known, Mr. Wolfe. I'll talk about anything you want me to, within reason."

Wolfe was frowning. "Not with any pledge of secrecy from me, sir. Neither tacit nor explicit. But I expose no man's privy affairs unnecessarily."

"If that's all I can get, I'll take that. What do you want to ask me?"

"Several things. First, where were you Tuesday afternoon from 4 to 6?"

There was no immediate reply. I could see there was movement inside the pocket where his fist was. To make things easier I horned in: "Which do you want, Scotch or rye?"

He looked at me and said sarcastically, "All the comforts of hell. If you mean it, Scotch. Don't spoon it out, you know."

I told him I wouldn't and trotted out and downstairs. In the ambush behind the draperies in the living room, on the shelves back of the bar, there were four brands to choose from. I long-armed cross the bar and got one, with a glass, poured out a generous triple, and returned to the library with it. It simply wasn't possible for Davis to keep his fingers from shaking as he took it. He only had to swallow twice. After a moment he put the glass down on the desk, and his fingers were steady.

He met Wolfe's eyes. "Tuesday afternoon," he said. "I was with Miss Karn from 3 o'clock until around 7."

"Where?"

"Driving. We went up to Connecticut and back. If the police have questioned her, that isn't what she told them, but I'm not telling the police, I'm telling you. If they question me, I'll tell them where I was, but I'll say I was alone."

"Did you stop to eat or drink?"

"No. We have no corroboration."

"That's too bad. Will you have some beer?"

Davis shuddered. "No!"

"I'm thirsty." Wolfe poured and put the bottle down. "You see, Mr. Davis, you may get into trouble. I doubt if the police have smelled you yet, but they certainly will if they keep on. They'll learn that you formed an attachment for Miss Karn a long while ago, and that when—"

"That's an old story. Back in 1935. How did you know about it?"

"I have men working for me. But the attachment still exists, doesn't it?"

"Certainly not."

"You were with Miss Karn Tuesday. You were with her last evening."

"We are friends. I'm a lawyer. She was consulting me."

Wolfe shook his head. "Please don't waste time like that. There are two pictures of her in your wallet, and Mr. Dawson has eight more scattered around his apartment."

Davis flushed in sudden anger, and his jaw stiffened. He shot me a glance that he should have been ashamed of, considering the fact that I had just saved his life with a triple Scotch.

"By God," he declared, "if I wasn't tied hand and foot—"

"You'd assault Mr. Goodwin. I know. I know too, I think, how reluctant you are to admit your attachment for Miss Karn as an item in a discussion like this. It is a vital necessity for you right now to keep your head clear and working efficiently, and that's difficult when a subject arises which causes your heart to pump an excess of blood. I'll go as easy as I can. But here's the material we have to deal with: You were passionately attached to Miss Karn. Noel Hawthorne saw her and liked her, and wanted her, and took her. Naturally you resented that. How much I don't know, but surely you resented it. However, either you continued some sort of association with her, or after a time you resumed association. Which?"

Davis didn't reply. Wolfe went on:

"I'm not thinking about murder now, I'm thinking about that will. Where was it drawn? In the office of Dunwoodie, Prescott & Davis. Where was it kept? In a vault in that office. Who benefited by it? Chiefly Miss Karn. Did she know that? Yes; Mr. Prescott let her read it shortly after it was drawn, having been instructed to do so by Mr. Hawthorne. Did you know that? I don't know. Did you?"

"No," said Davis curtly. "It was none of my business. Prescott drew it."

"But you have access to the vault?"

"I'm a lawyer, not a snoop, Mr. Wolfe."

"But isn't it plausible that Miss Karn told you about it? Couldn't you have learned it that way?"

"It may be plausible, but she didn't. I knew nothing, absolutely nothing, about the terms of that will until Miss Karn told me last night. Has Prescott told you I did?"

"Oh, no. No one has told me anything, really. They're all like you. I've sat in this confounded room over seven hours, and I know very little more than when I entered it. I don't resent it that each of you people has something to conceal—everybody in the world has—but it has never taken me so long to find a loose end. Let's start somewhere else. You say you are Miss Karn's friend and lawyer and she consults you. Did you advise her to come here this afternoon to negotiate with Mrs. Hawthorne?"

"No. Why?"

"Because she came."

"She came here?"

"Yes."

"How do you know? Did you see her?"

"No. Mr. Goodwin did. He had a little talk with her. Down in the living room. I thought perhaps—"

He chopped it off because the door suddenly opened. There was no knock, but it swung wide and Glenn Prescott marched in.

Chapter 12

The two counselors-at-law looked at each other. Prescott, having halted in his stride, advanced and said, "Hello, Gene." Davis nodded but didn't speak. I could see both their faces. Davis's exhibited vigilance and contempt; Prescott's, vigilance and a sort of exasperated solicitude.

"Relax!" Davis commanded. "Quit looking like the damned Salvation Army! I'm sober. These fellows jolted me sober. They know I was with Miss Karn last evening, and they know my name's Dawson on 11th Street. So I've been answering questions. Nothing indiscreet. Just where I was Tuesday afternoon and things like that."

Prescott said, "You're a fool. You were a fool to come here. You could have been kept out of this. It can't possibly be kept quiet longer than another day. When the papers start on it, and on you as a part of it—where are Dunwoodie, Prescott & Davis going to be?"

"The dear old firm," Davis sneered.

"Yes, Gene, the dear old firm. We've made it, but

it made us, too. You were headed for the top, you had
it in you. You still have. I'm a pretty good lawyer and
a hard worker, but you're a lot more than that. You're
one of the rare ones, the kind that makes history. I
don't need to tell you that. And now you don't even—
you come here and step into this—oh, my God."

He turned abruptly to Wolfe. "You've got us at
your mercy. What are you going to do? Hand it over to
the police?"

Wolfe shook his head. "No, sir. I might for a quid
pro quo, but the police have nothing I want. Sit down;
let's talk it over. I was just asking Mr. Davis if he
advised Miss Karn to come here to negotiate with
Mrs. Hawthorne."

"If he advised—" Prescott gawked. "Why did you
ask him that?"

Davis forestalled Wolfe's answer: "Because she
came! She was here!" He was on his feet, confronting
his partner. "And now I'm asking you! Did you bring
her here?"

"You're crazy, Gene. For God's sake, have a little
sense. I tell you, this is no time—"

"You brought her here!"

"You're crazy! Why would I—"

"I'm going to find out," Davis declared, and
tramped from the room.

We all stared at the open door which he had
disdained to close. Then Prescott said abruptly, "The
damned idiot," and out he went too. I was out of my
chair, asking hopefully:

"Do you want 'em?"

"No, Archie." Wolfe leaned back and sighed. "No,
thank you." He closed his eyes. "No, thank you."

"You're quite welcome," I said politely, and sat
down again without bothering to close the door. That
was merely one more example of my self-control.
Inwardly I was in a turmoil. I knew the signs. I knew
that tone of his. It was the first symptom of the
approach of a relapse. Unless I could bully him out of
it, or unless the murderer came in and confessed
within an hour, he would have a relapse as sure as ham
loves eggs. What made it so ticklish was the fact that
we weren't at home. If we had been at the office I
would have stood an even chance of jolting him loose,
but there on alien territory I wasn't so sure of myself.
So I don't know how long I might have sat there trying
to decide the best line to take, beyond the ten minutes
or so I did sit, if I hadn't heard footsteps stopping at
the doorway. I turned my head and saw it was the
butler.

"Speak," I said listlessly.

"Yes, sir. Mr. Dunn would like to see Mr. Wolfe in
the living room."

"Bring me a derrick." I waved him away. "You've
done your share. I'll get him there if I can."

He went. I waited a full minute and then demanded, "Did you hear that?"

"Yes."

"Well?"

No answer. I waited another minute. "Look here.
You are not in your own home. You came here of your
own volition. It's not Dunn's fault that this thing is
turning into a plate of sour hash, unless he killed
Hawthorne himself. He invited you here and you
came. Either go down and see what he wants, or let's
go home and starve."

He stirred, slowly opened his eyes, and pronounced a word in some foreign tongue which I have never bothered to ask him to translate, because it sounds as if it couldn't be printed anyway. He got out of his chair, and he moved toward the door. I followed.

We found they were having a convention in the living room. The delegates consisted of John Charles Dunn, Glenn Prescott, Osric Stauffer, a wiry little squirt whom I recognized as Detective-Lieutenant Bronson of the police, and a six-footer in a hot and dignified three-piece suit who looked concentrated and uncomfortable. By the introduction, made by Dunn, he was identified as Mr. Ritchie of the Cosmopolitan Trust Company, executor of Noel Hawthorne's estate.

Dunn also explained why we had been ousted from the library. The police had asked for permission to inspect the private papers of Hawthorne, most of which were in a safe built into the library wall, and the trust company had granted it, on condition that they should have a representative present. That was Mr. Ritchie. It was also thought desirable that Hawthorne's personal attorney should be there. That was Mr. Prescott. And to protect, if necessary, the confidential affairs of Daniel Cullen and Company, they wanted a man there too. That was Mr. Stauffer.

Bronson, Stauffer, Prescott and Ritchie marched off upstairs to open the safe. I thought to myself, they'll find another will as sure as water's wet, and then we'll have to solve the damn murder to get any fee at all.

John Charles Dunn was asking Wolfe if he had made any progress, and Wolfe was replying grumpily that he hadn't. I knew better than to try any badger-

ing in the presence of Dunn, but I thought I might as
well try something, so I crossed the room to where the
draperies were and pulled them open, thinking to
show Wolfe where I had found Stauffer in ambush.
But there was more than that there to show him, if he
had been beside me, though I nearly missed it. She
must have heard me, or seen me through a slit,
approaching. All I saw was the back of the gray gown,
and the back of her head, as she went through the door
in the right rear corner.

I called to Wolfe and Dunn, "Come here a minute!"

"What is it?"

"Come here and I'll show you." They crossed to
me. I held the curtain open. "I admit it's her house,
but it's a bad habit to get into anyhow. When I was in
here alone this morning, Mrs. Hawthorne suddenly
appeared from behind these drapes and then vanished. This is also the ambush I mentioned in that note
I gave you while she was in the library. And she was
in here just now. When I lifted the curtain she was
beating it through that door. Not that it seems to be
the answer to anything, but I thought you'd like to
know."

"You saw her leaving just now?"

"Yes, sir. Practicing, do you suppose?"

"I have no idea. As you say, it's her house. Since
she would have been quite welcome—what's the matter, Mr. Dunn?"

Dunn was looking queer. His jaw was working and
his eyes were bulging, though his stare seemed to be
directed nowhere in particular, certainly not at us. He
muttered something unintelligible and stared around

as if he expected to see something. Wolfe asked him again what was the matter.

"It was there!" he said, pointing to the chair the counterfeit Daisy had been sitting on when I found her with Naomi Karn. "We were right there!"

"Who were? When?"

"I was! With two men. To settle that Argentina loan. I came up from Washington to meet them, and wanted to keep the meeting secret. Noel was in Europe. I telephoned Daisy, and she said she wouldn't be at home that evening—she would instruct Turner to let us in. It's incredible! She didn't know who I was meeting or what it was about! Good God!"

"A chronic eavesdropper doesn't require any special inducement," said Wolfe dryly.

"She hid here and listened! She must have! And she told Noel—and he—" Dunn choked it off abruptly. In a moment he went on. "No, I'm wrong. I remember now. Daria—one of the men mentioned these curtains, and I got up and parted them and looked in here. It was empty. There wasn't much light, only what came from the opening in the curtains, but it was empty."

"Wait a minute," I told him. "I like this idea, let's hang onto it. She could have entered by that door after you looked behind the curtains. Better yet, she could have simply ducked behind the bar when she heard one of you mention the curtains."

Wolfe objected, "There's not enough room."

"Sure there's enough room." I was all for it. "Don't judge other people by yourself. Hell, I could hide there easily. Look, I'll give you a demonstration."

I stepped to the open end of the bar.

But the demonstration was never made. Sliding

behind the bar, I stumbled on something and nearly fell. I looked to see what it was, and a mouse ran up my spine. I stooped to see better, but the light was too dim, and I said, "There's a light switch on the wall. Turn it on."

Dunn did so. Wolfe, hearing my tone, inquired sharply, "What's the matter with you?"

I had to brace my knee against the edge of the bottom shelf so as not to kneel on her in that cramped space. After looking and feeling for a few seconds, I scrambled upright and told them, "It's Naomi Karn. Dead. Strangled with that blue linen wrap she was wearing tied around her throat."

Chapter 13

Wolfe grunted, compressed his lips, and glared at me ferociously, as if I had done it myself. John Charles Dunn showed admirable presence of mind. He didn't faint or scream. His face expressed shock and consternation, naturally, but almost immediately his jaw set and he moved, joined me at the end of the bar and looked in there at it. After a moment he looked at me.

"She's dead?"

"Yes, sir."

"You're sure."

"Yes, sir."

He put his hand on the edge of the bar for support. Then he moved again, not very steadily. I moved faster, got a chair from the other side of the draperies, and slid it behind him. He sat on it, gripped his knees with his fingers, and told the space in front of him, "This is the end of everything."

Wolfe said grimly, "Or the beginning. Archie, I want two minutes. In two minutes go up and notify Lieutenant Bronson."

I looked approvingly at his broad back as it passed through the curtains. I had no idea what he was going to do with the two minutes, but normal people aren't supposed to understand what geniuses are up to. I timed it by the second hand of my watch. Dunn sat there making no sound, gripping his knees and gazing at space. When the second hand had completed two revolutions, and was halfway around again for good measure, I told him, "You'd better stay here. You ought to breathe deeper. Take some deep breaths."

No one was in sight in the main hall, the stairs, or the upper corridor. I opened the door to the library and walked in. From the group around the desk, on which batches of papers were piled, four pairs of eyes turned my way in surprise. I was aware that the proper stunt was to summon the officer of the law, lead him downstairs and show it to him, and let nature take its course, but I was curious to see the expression on a couple of faces, so I announced distinctly:

"We have made a discovery downstairs. In the bar back of the drapes in the living room. Naomi Karn is there on the floor, dead."

I got nothing very definite, as usual. Stauffer merely gawked at me. Prescott merely jerked his head up and looked startled. Mr. Ritchie appeared to be annoyed. Lieutenant Bronson snapped at me, "Dead? Who's Naomi Karn?"

"A woman," I replied. "The one that inherited Hawthorne's pile. She has a thing fastened around her throat and her tongue is sticking out. Mr. Dunn is down there. You might as well go ahead and use that phone—"

He told the others brusquely, "You men stay here

and watch these papers," and me, "Come along," as he
went by headed for the door. I trotted behind, down
the stairs and through the entrance hall and living
room, circled around him to pull the drapery aside for
him to pass through, and told him, "There behind the
bar." Dunn was still on his chair. Bronson slid into
the narrow space and stooped over. Pretty soon he
straightened up again and spoke:

"I'm going to the library and use the phone. I'd
appreciate it, Mr. Dunn, if you'll kindly stay here until
I get back." He eyed me. "You're Goodwin, Nero
Wolfe's man."

"Right."

"Where's Wolfe?"

"He went somewhere upstairs, I guess. He sent
me to notify you."

"Was he with you when you found it?"

"Yes."

"How long ago was that?"

"Up to now? Oh, three-four minutes."

"Will you please stay at the front door while I'm
upstairs? No one is to leave the house."

"Sure, glad to."

I went with him as far as the main hall.

Considering the size of that house and the number
of its occupants, and in view of the restrictions and
complications that were to begin in about six minutes
with the arrival of the first contingent of city employees in a radio car, there is no telling when I would have
realized what Nero Wolfe had done with that two
minutes he had said he wanted, if it hadn't been for my
habit of looking in all directions. But possibly there
was some faint suspicion in the back of my mind, or I

wouldn't have opened the entrance door and stepped out for a look around, and noticed that something was missing. I craned my neck for an inspection of the cars parked in that short block, and verified it. Absolutely, the sedan was gone. It wasn't where I had parked it, and it wasn't there at all.

But of course Wolfe hadn't driven off in it himself, since, although theoretically he knew how to drive, he would have collapsed with terror at the mere idea. But since Naomi Karn hadn't left the house, and therefore Orrie Cather was still on the job, Wolfe would have known that a chauffeur was available. I sent my gaze in the other direction, toward the areaway across the street where I had found Orrie. He wasn't there. He wasn't in sight. That cinched it. If Orrie had still been around he would have had an eye on that entrance, and would have seen me, and would have made himself visible.

I stood and let the conviction seep into my soul. "I can't say it any better than that," I muttered bitterly to myself. "Normal people aren't supposed to understand what geniuses are up to. If only I had sunk my toe in his fundament as he went through those curtains."

A siren sounded from around the corner, a little green car came curving into 67th, jerked to a stop at the curb, and two men in uniform hopped out and started for me. I had left the door ajar, and swung it open for them to enter.

That was the beginning of as dreary and unprofitable a six-hour stretch as I've ever struggled through. By midnight I was ready to bite holes in the windows. On account of the kind of individuals involved, by their being on the premises if by nothing else, the whole damn city and county payroll showed up sooner or later, from the commissioner and the district attorney on down. Wherever you stepped it was on a toe. As far as picking up any items for myself was concerned, I had about as much chance as a poodle in a pack of bloodhounds. Throughout the entire session, about every ten minutes someone came up to me and asked me where Nero Wolfe was. That alone got so obnoxious I had to grit my teeth to keep from slugging some high official.

Soon after the first squad men arrived, Lieutenant Bronson had me in the music room. That interview was brief and unimportant; about all he wanted was the details of our finding the body. I gave it to him complete and straight. I wouldn't have minded keeping our knowledge of Daisy's addiction to eavesdropping for the firm's private use, in case it should come in handy, but I had to give a reason for my looking behind the bar, and it was too risky to invent one, since he had already had a talk with Dunn, and Dunn had probably told him just how it was. So I did too. When it was over he chased me upstairs. I was to remain and so forth. The first thing he asked me, and the last, was "Where's Wolfe?"

I went in the library and saw there was no one there but Ritchie of the Cosmopolitan Trust, sitting looking glum and offended, and a dick I didn't know, so I went out again. Prescott came trotting down the hall, saw me, stopped beside me, glanced around, and asked in an undertone, "Where's Wolfe?"

"I don't know. Don't ask me again. I don't know."

"He must have—"

"I don't know!"

"Don't talk so loud. We've got to keep Gene Davis out of this." He was urgent, pleading. "No one saw him but Wolfe and you and me. I'm sure if Wolfe were here I could convince him. They mustn't know Gene was here. When they ask you—"

"Not a chance. You'd better compose your faculties. The butler let him in."

"But I can tell Turner, I can persuade him—"

"No, sir. There are about nine things the cops won't find out from me, but that isn't one of them. Take my advice and never conspire with a butler."

He grabbed my lapel. "But I tell you, if they learn Davis was here, if they once get started after him—"

"I can't help it, Mr. Prescott. Sorry. No one likes to keep a secret from a cop any more than I do, but that would be just begging for trouble. I'll do this much, I'll make them ask for it, I won't volunteer it—"

Footsteps from above, on the next flight of stairs, interrupted me. It was Andy Dunn coming down. He caught sight of us, and told Prescott his father would like to see him in Mrs. Hawthorne's room. Prescott looked at me half angrily and half pleadingly, and I shook my head. Andy addressed me:

"Dad would like to see Nero Wolfe too. Where is he?"

I answered that one, and they went off, and I moseyed to the end of the corridor and sat on a bench. After a while I started down to the main floor to look over fresh arrivals, but got shooed back up before I touched bottom, and went to the library and appropriated a comfortable chair. It was while I was there that a maid came around with sandwiches and milk and ginger ale, and I took enough to last a while. The next scene I had any part in was when a squad man appeared and said that Mr. Dunn himself had suggested that everyone in the house submit to having their fingerprints taken, and the others had agreed, and he was prepared to oblige me. Having just wasted a lot of breath trying to persuade the dick on guard in the library that it would be conducive to the interest of law and order to let me use the phone, I was sore. I refused, and said my prints were on file downtown, since I was a licensed detective. He said he knew that, but it would be more convenient to take them with the others. I said it would be more convenient for me to go home and go to bed, since it was after dark, and he could go sit on a trylon. I admit I was churlish, but so were they. All I wanted to do was phone the house and ask Fritz how he was.

I got tired of the library and wandered out to the hall again. The three kids were there, Celia and Sara sitting on a bench and Andy standing in front of them, talking in whispers. They looked at me and stopped whispering, but had nothing to say to me. Not wanting to interfere with any childish secrets, I went on up to the next floor. The third door on the left was standing wide open, and a glance through as I passed by revealed May and June seated side by side on a sofa. I noted that May had exchanged the old faded gown for something fresher, a white dress with pink spots. At the street end of the hall was a window, and I went there and stood a while, looking down at the confusion outdoors. Parked cars were solid at the curb on both sides, and streams of both pedestrian and vehicle traffic were being kept moving by a scattering

of cops. The radio certainly is a blessing for people
who like their meat fresh. Standing there surveying
the bustling scene, I turned from time to time at the
sound of footsteps behind me, but it was never anything more exciting than one of the inmates en route
to or from the stairs, a dick who was obviously a
messenger from the ground floor.

On two occasions, however, the footsteps kept
coming until they got me. The first time it was Osric
Stauffer. He gazed at me from ten paces off, evidently
decided I was the customer he was calling on, and
came clear up to me before he spoke.

"I understand Nero Wolfe isn't around. If you—"

"I don't know where he is," I said firmly.

"So Dunn tells me. But if you—the fact is, I was
looking for you before—when they sent for me—"

I wouldn't have said that at that moment he was
living up to much of anything. He was close to pitiful.
He was trying to keep from trembling but couldn't,
and his voice sounded as if his throat was badly in need
of oiling.

I said, "Here I am, but I'm in one hell of a temper.
You don't look very happy yourself."

"I suppose—I don't. This ghastly—right here—
with all of us here."

"Yeah, sure. It wouldn't have been so bad if she'd
been all alone in the house."

I was hoping he'd resent that enough to quit
looking pathetic, but his mind was too occupied even
to realize it was an ill-timed jest. All he did was move
ten inches closer to me and speak in a lower and more
urgent tone:

"Do you want to earn a thousand dollars?"

"Certainly. Don't you?"

"For nothing," he said. "Really nothing. I've just had a talk with Skinner, the district attorney. I didn't tell him about my being behind those curtains—you know—when you came in and saw me. It would have been—it would have sounded too damned silly." He pulled one of the poorest imitations of a jolly little laugh in my long experience. "It was silly—the silliest thing I ever did in my life. I'll give you—I mean, when they question you—if you forget you saw me there— you'll earn a thousand dollars—just to save me the embarrassment—I haven't got that much with me, but you can take my word—"

He ran down. I grinned at him. "No spik Eenglis."

"But I tell you—"

"No, brother. If you didn't kill her, you'd be overpaying me. If you did, you're a piker. But if it will relieve your mind any to know it, my rule is never to give a cop anything to hold if it's something I might want back. There are a few pieces of information I intend to keep at least temporarily for my private use—since Nero Wolfe has retired—and the fact that you sneak into bars in private houses is one of them."

"But—you say temporarily—I've got to know—"

"That's the best I can do for you, and don't offer me any more pennies. My mother told me not to accept money from strangers."

He was by no means satisfied. It appeared that what he wanted was an anti-aggression bloc with unilateral action rigidly excluded, and he was pretty stubborn about it. I don't know how I would have got rid of him if John Charles Dunn hadn't come down the hall, caught sight of him, and taken him off into a room. For, I calculated, a report of his session with Skinner.

The second approach to my anchorage by the window was just after I had returned from a trip to the library to get an ash tray. This time I wasn't being sought for; at least it didn't look like it. Sara and Celia and Andy came up together from the floor below, and saw me, and Sara said something to the other two which seemed to start an argument. They hissed back and forth for a couple of minutes, and then Andy and Celia entered at the open door through which I had seen May and June seated talking, and Sara trotted up to me. As she approached I observed:

"I see they haven't arrested you yet."

"Of course not. Why should they?"

"They're apt to. If you confess to enough crimes and misdemeanors, you'll hit on one they can't prove you didn't do."

"Don't be so darned smart." She sat down on the bench that was there. "This—all this—has gone to my legs. I can't stand up. It stimulates me like cocktails on an empty stomach. I suppose when I go to bed, if I go to bed at all, I'll be crushed and I'll lie and stare at the dark and be miserable, and I may even throw up, but now it just makes my legs weak and excites my brain. I have got a brain."

"So has a cricket." I sat beside her. "You remind me of a cricket."

"That might interest me some day, but it doesn't now. Andy was disagreeing with me, and of course Celia was on his side. Heavens, are they hooked! Andy says that the family is in danger, in horrible danger, and that we ought to stick together and trust no one."

"Whereas you're in favor of trusting? Who, me?"

"Not trust exactly. Trust doesn't enter into it that I can see. I was merely going to tell you something that happened this afternoon."

"I must warn you, Miss Dunn, that after that confession of yours I'll suspect anything you say. I doubt if I'll even take the trouble to check up on it."

She made an unladylike noise. "Nobody's asking you to check up on it. Only it happened, and I'm going to tell you. I told dad, and I don't think he even heard me. I told Mr. Prescott, and he said, 'Yes, yes,' and patted me on the shoulder. I told Andy and Celia, and I swear to heaven they think I made it up. Why the dickens would I make it up that somebody stole my camera?"

"Oh. Is that what happened?"

"Yes, and whoever it was took two rolls of film too. You see, we came down to New York from the country Wednesday morning. Dad had to go back to Washington, but the famous Hawthorne girls decided the rest of us should camp in this house until after the funeral, and Aunt Daisy said all right." She shivered. "Doesn't that veil give you the creeps?"

I said it did.

She went on. "It certainly does me. When we got here Wednesday morning, I went to my room on 19th Street and brought a bag of clothes. I had nothing with me in the country because Mr. Prescott took me right up there from the shop. Then after the funeral he read the will to us and all this mess started. So we all stayed here Thursday night and again last night. I've been sleeping in that room with Celia." She pointed to the second door on the left. "And this afternoon I noticed my camera was gone. Somebody stole it."

"Or maybe borrowed it."

"No, I've asked everyone, including the servants. Besides, they went through my bag too, messed it all up, and took two rolls of film."

"Maybe a servant did it. She wouldn't admit it when you asked, you know. Very few people have a confession complex like you. Or maybe Aunt Daisy is a kleptomaniac as well as an eavesdropper."

"How do you know she's an eavesdropper?"

"I've seen her at work."

"Have you? I never have. Andy says if my camera was stolen it must have been by a member of the family and the best thing I can do is keep my mouth shut about it."

"That sounds sensible. If it ever comes to a vote, my ballot goes to Aunt Daisy. Were the two rolls of film—Ah, company's coming."

It was a dick I didn't know, looking stern and important. He came up to us.

"Archie Goodwin? Inspector Cramer wants you downstairs."

Chapter 14

The stage selected for my personal appearance was the music room. Some magazines and books had been cleared off of a large table, and at the far side of it sat District Attorney Skinner, in his shirt sleeves with his hair rumpled up. Inspector Cramer, with his coat and vest, which I had never seen him without, was on the piano bench. At one end of the table was Police Commissioner Hombert, looking tired and frustrated, and at the other end was a detective with a notebook. The chair ready for me was placed properly, so they could all see my face, with the light shining in my eyes.

I sat down and said, "This is quite a compliment, all three of you like this."

Cramer blurted at me, "That'll do! This is one time we want no gags! And no hedging! We want answers and that's all!"

"Sure, I understand that," I said in a hurt voice, "but I come in here expecting to be questioned by a sergeant or maybe a lieutenant, and when I actually find that the three most brilliant—"

"All right, Goodwin," Skinner snapped. "You can speak a piece for us some other time. Where's Nero Wolfe?"

"I don't know. I've told at least a million—"

"I know you have. We're told at his house that he's not there. He left here immediately after you found the body. Where did he go?"

"Search me."

"Where did he say he was going?"

"He didn't say. If you want facts, I'm out. If you want an opinion, you can have mine."

"Let's have it."

"I think he went home to dinner."

"Nonsense. He was here on an important case, with important clients, and a murder was committed right under his nose. Do you expect me to believe— not even Nero Wolfe would be eccentric enough—"

"I don't know about eccentric enough, but he was hungry enough. He had a bum lunch." I made a gesture. "You say you were told he isn't home. Naturally. He doesn't want to be disturbed. You might pry the door open with a search warrant, but what would you write on it? If you've asked questions around here, you must have discovered by now that he was upstairs in the library from 10:30 this morning until just before we discovered the body. He didn't leave it once. So what do you want him for anyway?"

Commissioner Hombert barked, "One thing we want is to ask him where and when he saw Naomi Karn today and what was said."

"He didn't see her today."

"We want to know the terms of the agreement he

made with her on behalf of his clients. We want to see the agreement."

"There isn't any. He didn't make any."

"I choke on that," Cramer declared bluntly. "If she made no agreement, signed nothing, Hawthorne's fortune belonged to her when she died, and Wolfe's clients are out of luck."

"And," I suggested, "whoever inherits from her is in luck. Had you thought of that?"

Hombert growled. Cramer looked startled. Skinner demanded, "And who is that? Who inherits from her?"

"I haven't the slightest idea. Not me."

"You're pretty fresh, aren't you, Goodwin?"

"Yes, sir. I resent being corraled up there with the herd for four hours. You could have taken me first as well as last. I know why you did it." I nodded at the pile of notes on the table. "You wanted to toss my lies right back at me. Go ahead and try."

But they wasted an hour peering into empty holes before they got to that part. When and where had I first seen Naomi Karn. Ditto Wolfe. Exactly what had happened, and what had been said, when I went to her apartment to get her the day before. Then the previous visitation of the Hawthornes and auxiliaries. What had April said. What had May said. What had June said. Had anyone threatened anyone. Then the talk with Naomi after the others had left. I tried to be obliging, but of course there were certain details that I regarded as inappropriate for the detective to have in his notebook, such as Naomi's calling Stauffer Ossie and Daisy Hawthorne's attack on the integrity of our clients, and I excluded those. Another thing I ne-

glected to mention was the Davis-Dawson episode
that morning. I merely said that Wolfe got a phone call
from Dunn around 9:30 and came to 67th Street, and
that I joined him there about an hour later. Then I
pulled a sheet of paper from my pocket and handed it
across to Skinner.

"I thought a timetable might simplify it," I told
him, "so I typed one on a machine up in the library
while I was awaiting your pleasure."

Hombert and Cramer got up and went to have a
look at it, one over each shoulder of the district
attorney. While they were digesting it I glanced over
the carbon copy I had kept for myself:

10:45	Joined Wolfe, Dunn & wife in library.
11:10	Butler announced Skinner, Cramer & Hombert calling on Dunn.
11:30	Phoned Durkin, Panzer & Keems. Sara Dunn came.
12:10	April, Celia & Stauffer.
12:30	Those three left. Panzer & Keems came, got instructions, and left.
1:10	Lunch.
2:15	Cramer came.
2:35	He left. Daisy H. came.
2:40	Durkin came.
2:42	I went outdoors and spoke to Orrie. Re-entered house and saw Naomi Karn in living room.
2:50	Durkin left.
3:10	I went downstairs and had short talk with Naomi Karn and returned to library.
4:55	Phone call from Panzer.

5:00 Daisy H. left.
5:05 I went to living room. Naomi Karn not there. Eugene Davis was. Took him to library.
5:40 Prescott came.
5:45 Davis & Prescott left.
5:55 Butler came. Dunn wanted Wolfe in living room. Wolfe & I went.
6:05 Bronson, Stauffer, Prescott & Ritchie went upstairs, leaving Dunn, Wolfe & me in living room.
6:11 Found body.

It looked all right. The few little items I had left out, such as Daisy's first draperies act, Sara's asking to see Wolfe, the counterfeit Daisy and her disappearance, and Stauffer's ambush, were all things they couldn't be expected to get from other sources.

"It's nice to have this," said Skinner. "Thank you very much." So he was going to try being oily. "Now just tell me what Wolfe was discussing with Mr. and Mrs. Dunn."

That started the second hour.

I had had plenty of time to get my mind in order, so it went along without much friction. Having ruled out Sara's confession and Daisy's story of the cornflower and a few other things I gave them enough to account for the afternoon. Naturally there were a few little clashes, the most serious one arising from Skinner's suggestion that it would be a good plan for me to turn over my notes of the various interviews. I told him they were Nero Wolfe's property and if he got them at all it would have to be from Wolfe himself.

They yapped some about that and Hombert got pretty unpleasant, but the notes stayed in my pocket. After that they calmed down again, and later even did me the honor to ask my opinion on a technical point. The police, they said, had seen the bar only when it was lit by electricity, whereas I had been there when the only light came from the little window in one corner, and only a moment after Daisy Hawthorne had left by the rear door. Mrs. Hawthorne had admitted to them that she had been there and that I had seen her leave. She had stated that, being reluctant to appear before people wearing that veil, she often entered the bar from the rear to observe callers from the shelter of the curtains; that she had done so today when she had been told that Ritchie and Bronson had come to inspect Hawthorne's private papers; that she had been there only a few minutes when my approach caused her to retreat; and that she had seen nothing on the floor behind the bar. With the light as it was in there at that time, did I think she could have entered by the door and failed to see the body?

I said yes, the light had been so dim that even when I stooped right over the body I had barely been able to tell who it was.

They skated around a while longer, and then Skinner sprung one on me that I had been expecting ever since I entered. It had in fact been on my tongue a couple of times to anticipate it, but I had decided there was no sense in depriving them of a little pleasure along with their work. So I concealed my grin when Skinner began a build-up for it.

He said casually, "One point that bothers us is that no one heard any outcry, not even the servants at the rear of this floor, and there wasn't the slightest sign of a struggle. Miss Karn seems to have been healthy and fairly sturdy. But apparently she didn't call for help and she offered no resistance to speak of."

"That's surprising," I agreed. "We didn't hear anything up in the library."

"I was just going to ask if you did."

"Nope. Of course, in cases of strangulation you'll often find that the victim was first rendered helpless by a blow or a drug or something. Your M.E. could tell you. And by the way, that reminds me of something I forgot to mention, while Davis was up there with us I offered to get him a drink because he looked like he could use one, and I went to the bar and poured about half a pint from a bottle of MacNeal's Diamond Label."

Cramer glared at me and snorted. "The hell you did." Hombert only snorted. Skinner said dryly, "Some day, Goodwin, you're going to pull one of those cute ones and it'll fly right back in your face."

"Gosh, that wasn't cute," I protested. "To be honest, I was worried. I saw that bruise on her head which must have come from a good hard blow. The handiest thing around there to strike a blow with, enough to put her out at one crack, was one of those bottles, especially if the murderer approached through the bar and the draperies, which seemed likely. If he did that, of course he would wipe his prints from the bottle before he put it back. But my prints were there, nice fresh ones, on that bottle of MacNeal's. Would you fellows find them? That's what had me worried stiff. You might possibly miss them. But probably you wouldn't. So I finally decided the only thing to do was to come clean and tell you exactly—"

"Shut up and beat it!" Cramer growled. "Why in the name of God 40,000 people get killed in automobile accidents every year and not one of them is you—take him out, Grier." That to the dick who had brought me in and who was on a chair by the door. "Go home and if Nero Wolfe's there tell him—don't tell him anything. I'll see him. I'll see you too. Stay where I can find you."

"Right." I got up. "Good night, gentlemen, and good luck. You can imagine how I felt when I realized that when I reached across the bar for that bottle of MacNeal's the body was right there—already there on the floor, dead—must have been—okay, I'm going, sorry if I irritated you—"

Grier followed me out and told the cop at the entrance door to let me through to freedom. Outside another pair of cops looked me over as I went by. There was still a row of P.D. cars parked at the curb. I walked to the corner and flagged a taxi. On the way downtown the driver wanted to chat about the murder, but the best I had to offer was ill-natured grunts.

I inserted my key and turned it and the knob, but the door opened two inches and stopped. The chain was on. So I leaned on the bell. In a second there were steps in the hall, and Fritz's eye was at the crack, peering at me.

"Ah, Archie?" He sounded relieved. "Are you alone?"

"No, I've got a machine-gun squad. Open up!"

He did so. I left the closing to him and proceeded. The office was dark. I entered the kitchen. It was

illuminated and smelled good as usual, and the French
newspaper Fritz had been reading was on a chair. He
trotted in and I confronted him.

"What time did Wolfe get home?"

"At 6:40. There's some duckling left, and some
cheese cake, if you—"

"No, thanks. I had some lovely sandwiches." I got
the jug from the refrigerator and poured a glass of
milk. "What time did he go to bed?"

"Soon after eleven. He said he was tired. He ate
with me in the kitchen, not to have a light in the dining
room, because he said the police were after him. Is he
in danger, Archie? Is it perhaps that we—"

"Sure he's in danger. Gulosity. Forget it. What the
dickens is that thing?"

I went closer to inspect it: a branch of something a
foot long, with a dozen twigs on it, a lot of little dark
green leaves, and many tiny thorns that looked sharp,
there on top of the low cabinet in a vase of water. Fritz
said he didn't know what it was; that Fred Durkin had
brought it and Wolfe had put it in the vase, with some
remark about ripening the seeds.

"Oh," I said, "then it must be a clue. Fred's a
wonder for collecting clues. I'll bet a nickel those little
stickers are Haw thorns. So it's a haw. Haw haw.
What time did Fred report?"

"About half past ten. He had quite a few clues in a
bag. And Saul came a little earlier and talked with Mr.
Wolfe. Also Johnny telephoned." Fritz glanced at the
pad which he kept beside the phone. "At 10:46—Oh,
here, something for you—" He took a piece of paper
from under the pad and handed it to me.

I looked at it.

> *Archie:*
>
> *I am not at home.*
>
> *N. W.*

I tossed it in the trash basket. "Haw haw haw haw," I observed, and went up to bed.

In the morning I half expected a summons to the bedroom when Fritz returned from delivering the breakfast tray, but there was none. I thought, all right, if the big buffalo wants to pretend it's just another Sunday morning I can too, and settled down in the kitchen to enjoy my anchovy omelet with a half a dozen pictures and three full pages of text regarding the Dunn-Hawthorne-Stauffer-Karn affair in the morning paper. Someone in Rockland County had talked, and the suspicion of foul play in Hawthorne's death was also loose, so it was a regular picnic.

Any fear that Wolfe had actually dived into a relapse was removed a little after nine o'clock, when Orrie Cather and Fred Durkin arrived simultaneously and told me they had been instructed to report and await orders. I was plenty relieved, but I was still determined that if communication was going to be re-established it wouldn't be through any advances by me. I knew he was up in the plant rooms because I had heard his elevator. Then I took a step. A phone call came from Inspector Cramer. I talked with him, and hung up, and buzzed the plant rooms on the inside wire. Wolfe answered.

I addressed him formally. "Good morning, sir. Inspector Cramer of the homicide squad just phoned that he was up all night, he wants to see you, and he will be here probably a little after twelve. He is working on a murder case. There are two kinds of detectives that work on homicides. One kind hastens to the scene of a murder. The other kind hastens away from it. Inspector Cramer is the first kind."

"I said in that note that I'm not at home."

"You can't continue being not at home indefinitely. Are there any orders for Fred and Orrie?"

"No. Have them wait."

The receiver went dead.

An hour later, at the customary time, eleven o'clock, his elevator descended and he entered the office. I waited until he was holding his chair down and then stated to him:

"I see you intend to brazen it out. I admit nothing is to be gained by a prolonged controversy. All I say is, that was the most preposterous goddam performance in the entire history of the investigation of crime. That's all. Now for my report—"

"There was nothing preposterous about it. It was the only sensible—"

"You couldn't sell me that in a thousand years. Do you want my report?"

He sighed, leaned back, and half closed his eyes. He looked as fresh as a daisy, and about as shame-faced as a fan dancer. "Go ahead."

I gave it to him, complete, from memory, for I had made no notes. It took quite a while. He asked no questions and let me go to the end without any interruption. When I was through he said again, sat up, and rang for beer.

"It's hopeless," he declared. "You say they sent for you last? They had interviewed all the others?"

"I think so. Certainly most of them. I think all of them."

"It's hopeless. I mean for us. With tenacity and perseverance the police may break that circle, but I doubt it. It's welded too tight. They were all there in the country when Hawthorne was killed. They were all in that house when Miss Karn died. Too many of them. I might get the truth if I worked hard enough for it, but what would I do with it? Could I establish it? How? They don't want it, not even Dunn himself, though he thinks he does. And I don't want it myself if I can't use it. Especially at the price it would cost. Do I?"

"No, sir. But you could use a little deposit at the bank."

"I'm aware of that. But the death of Miss Karn makes it impossible to proceed even with the matter of the will. If she left a will herself—pfui! It's hopeless."

"Then what are Fred and Orrie sitting around for, at eight bucks a day? Local color?"

"No. I'm hanging on until I see Mr. Cramer. And others who'll be coming before the day's out. Two or three of them, I fancy, will want to see me."

"They sure will," I agreed. "Stauffer will want to bribe you. Daisy will want to sell you another cornflower. And of course Sara will want you to recover her camera. Oh, I forgot to mention that. She told me somebody stole her camera."

"Miss Dunn? When?"

"Last night just before they sent for me. I mean she told me then. It was yesterday afternoon she missed the camera from her room there in the house. Also two rolls of film she had in her bag or suitcase.

She said she asked everybody, including the servants, but no soap."

"Had the rolls of film been exposed?"

"I don't know. I didn't get a chance to ask her, because we were interrupted by Cramer sending for me."

"Get Miss Dunn. At once."

I stared. "She didn't offer any reward for its recovery."

"Get her, please! This is our first chance to pick up something that was dropped. It may be only a thieving servant, but I doubt it, with the films gone too. Do the others know she told you about it?"

"Andy and Celia do. I can't phone her, because the cops—"

"I didn't say phone her! I said get her! Bring her here!"

Chapter 15

O n the way uptown in the roadster I devised two or three nifty ruses for getting the professional fiend off the premises without annoying either cops or family, but by the time I arrived at 67th Street I had decided that direct action was the quickest and most feasible. A flatfoot out front who was keeping sightseers on the move seemed to think I wasn't needed there, but I talked my way through him, pushed the button, and was admitted by the butler. I asked for Mr. Dunn.

In a few minutes Dunn joined me in the living room. He looked as if he hadn't slept for a week and never expected to again. I told him Nero Wolfe had beat it the day before in order to pursue certain activities without restriction from the police, that he was at home and was on the job. The poor guy was so punch drunk that he couldn't even ask an intelligent question. He sort of sputtered that he didn't see what Wolfe could do, he hoped he could do something but what, it was beyond remedy, did Wolfe have any idea . . .

I had never expected to find myself patting John Charles Dunn on the shoulder to buck him up. But I did, and spent twenty minutes with him trying to persuade him that Nero Wolfe would roll the clouds away and the sun would shine. That was partly in preparation for telling him his daughter Sara was wanted in Wolfe's office, but when I finally did so he wasn't even curious as to why we wanted her. He had been under a strain for months, and now this had about finished him. He sent the butler for her, and in no time I had her out of the house and in the roadster.

But when I got to Wolfe's house I drove on past without slowing down, eighty yards or so, and then rolled to the curb and stopped. Sara Dunn looked at me.

"What's the matter? That's it back there, isn't it?"

"Yeah, but that car in front is Inspector Cramer's, and what he don't know won't hurt him. We'll wait here till he goes."

"Oh. Darn it anyway. It would be simply marvelous, doings like this, if it wasn't so—if it wasn't my own f-family—"

"All right, sister. I'll teach you to be a detective some day." I patted her hand because her lip was trembling and I didn't want her crying, but it only made it tremble more, so I quit. I twisted around on the seat to get a good view of the rear through the window, and after a while, ten minutes or so, saw Cramer emerge and start down the stoop. I started the car, went around the block and into 35th again, and parked in front of the house.

I was about half-bored as I sat and listened to Wolfe starting in on her. Not that I was too dumb to be able to figure that if her camera and films had been stolen it might have been done by somebody to conceal something connected either with the will or with the murder. Of course that was a possibility. But I was cold on it for two reasons. First, on account of Sara's intimate disclosures when she confessed she had betrayed her father and slaughtered her uncle. I wanted proof that anything had been stolen at all. Second, although she was loony she wasn't stupid, and she must have realized that if anybody was going to be exposed by investigating the theft of the camera it could only be someone in her family or close to it. I never knew until the following winter, when I took her to a show one evening, that she thought all the time she knew who had killed Hawthorne and Naomi Karn both, and it was someone she didn't like.

Apparently Wolfe was taking the larceny seriously. He went into all the details, making sure she had actually left the camera in the bedroom, and the films in the suitcase; also, he wanted to know exactly how and when she had informed each of the others of her loss, and what they had said and how they had acted. She gave him all that without any visible reluctance or hesitation, except when he asked about Osric Stauffer. At that she balked for a moment, and then said she hadn't mentioned it to Stauffer. Wolfe asked her why, and she said because she wouldn't have believed anything Stauffer told her, so there was no use asking him.

Why, did she know Stauffer to be a liar?

No, but she didn't like his mouth, or his eyes either, and she wouldn't trust him.

Wolfe's brows went up a little. "Am I to assume,

Miss Dunn, that you think Mr. Stauffer stole your camera?"

She shook her head. "I wouldn't expect you to assume anything. I thought detectives didn't assume, I thought they deduced."

Wolfe grunted. "They do if they can. They try. Anyhow, I doubt if your dislike for Mr. Stauffer's mouth and eyes will convict him of anything." He glanced up at the clock, which said a quarter past one. "Let's try another path briefly before we have lunch. You say the two rolls of film in the suitcase had not been exposed. Then if what the thief was after was exposed film, he presumably took those two cartons on a chance, being in too much of a hurry to investigate there in your bedroom. And the only exposed film he got was the one that was still in the camera."

Sara shook her head again. "He didn't get any at all. There was none in the camera."

Wolfe frowned. "You said that the picture you took in this office Friday afternoon finished a roll, and that that roll was in the camera when you put it in the bedroom."

"I know I did. But you didn't let me go on. I removed the film from the camera Friday evening and took it to a drugstore to be developed. That was when I bought the two rolls—"

"Confound it," Wolfe snapped, "where are they?"

"Where are what?"

"The pictures!"

"I suppose at the drugstore." She fished in her handbag and got out a piece of cardboard. "Here's the check. He said they'd be ready the next evening—that was yesterday—"

"May I have that, please?" Wolfe extended a hand. "Thank you. Archie, call Fred and Orrie."

I went to the kitchen, where they were picking their teeth after a repast, and brought them in. Wolfe handed the check to Orrie and told him:

"That's for some snapshots. The address is on it. Miss Dunn left the film Friday evening. Take the roadster; I want the pictures and the film as soon as possible. I think I do. I'll know when I look at them."

"Yes, sir." They went.

Wolfe got up and stood scowling at Sara. "Would you mind removing your hat, Miss Dunn? I deduce the thing is a hat, because it's on your head. Thank you. I don't like restaurant conventions in my dining room."

The occasions have been rare when I have known the pressure of business to cause Wolfe to accelerate the tempo of a meal, but it did that Sunday. For the first half hour, while the melon and cutlets and broccoli were being disposed of, he maintained the usual easy balance of consumption and conversation; but during the service of the salad Fred and Orrie returned, were admitted by Fritz, and left to wait in the office. I got two grins in a row, the first when Wolfe broke his rule excluding any reference to business from the dining room by asking Fritz to ask Orrie if he had got what he went for, and the second when the salad dressing was ready in six minutes instead of the usual eight. The peeling and slicing of peaches would have hung up a record, too, if I had clocked it; and while I couldn't have called his step nimble as he led the way back into the office, it certainly didn't drag any.

He took the envelope from Orrie and told him and

Fred to wait in front, sat down and shook the pictures
out onto the desk, and spoke to Sara:

"You'll have to tell me what these are, Miss Dunn."

I started to move a chair up for her, but she waved
me away and sat on the arm of his, balancing herself
with her hand on his shoulder. He grimaced but took
it. I completed the group by moving to his other side,
for the pictures were so small—the usual miniatures of
a Leitax—that I had to get close to make them out.

There were thirty-six of them altogether, and most
of them were pretty good shots. Wolfe discarded the
majority the first time through—a bunch that had no
discernible connection with Hawthornes or Dunns
alive or dead, including nine or ten she had taken
Monday evening at the World's Fair. The remainder
he examined with his magnifying glass, asking Sara
about them, and marking on the back of each the
place, date and hour it had been taken. Finally he
returned thirty of them, together with the films, to
the envelope, laid it aside, and concentrated on the six
that were left. Sara got tired of balancing on the chair
arm and resumed her former seat at the end of the
desk. I got my own glass and did some concentrating
myself, studying each of the six pictures in turn as he
laid one down to pick up another one, and starting
over again when my first tour disclosed nothing star-
tling.

Sara's information was that Number One had been
taken about nine o'clock Wednesday morning. May
Hawthorne was exhibiting one of the crows which had
been shot the day before by Noel Hawthorne and
which Titus Ames had just found in a meadow; Mrs.
Dunn was looking at it curiously while April Haw-

thorne regarded it with revulsion. Sara had snapped them before they knew it, and a moment later, hearing a noise behind her on the terrace, had turned, seen Daisy with her veil standing there, and snapped her too. That was Number Two.

Number Three had been taken shortly after six o'clock Tuesday afternoon, when Sara had emerged from the shop where she worked and found Glenn Prescott there with his car waiting to take her to the country. Number Four had been taken some three hours earlier the same afternoon, Tuesday. Sara had gone up Park Avenue to deliver a vase to a customer in a hurry, and had taken her camera along as usual. She had seen, crossing the sidewalk, the woman whom she had seen before, months previously, entering Hartlespoon's in the company of her Uncle Noel; and the door of the car which the woman headed for was being opened by a man whom she recognized, though she had not seen him for years, as Eugene Davis, the law partner of Glenn Prescott. She took a shot as the woman was approaching the car.

Number Five had been taken Wednesday morning, not long before Number One. She had gone through the woods for a look at the spot where her Uncle Noel had met his death, and finding her father, her brother, and Osric Stauffer there, had earned remonstrances from all three of them by snapping a picture of the scene. Number Six, of course, needed no explanation. It was the one she had taken with a flash there in Wolfe's office Friday afternoon.

My glass was as good as Wolfe's, and so I had no handicap with regard to details, but after completing my third inspection of everything I could find, I passed. As far as I was concerned, the only thing those snaps proved was that Sara was handy with a Leitax. I went to my desk and sat down.

Wolfe was through, too. He was leaning back in his chair with his eyes closed. I watched him. His lips were moving, pushing out and thickening, and then closing in again to make a thin line. I watched him, and wondered whether he really had something or was only bluffing. If he was bluffing it could have been only for my benefit, for Sara Dunn didn't know what that movement of his lips meant.

Suddenly she demanded, "Well? Are you deducing something?"

His lips stopped moving. His eyelids raised to make slits, enough to see her through, and after a moment he slowly shook his head.

"No," he murmured at her, "the deducing is finished. That was simple. The hard part of it—"

"But you—" She stiffened, staring at him. "You don't mean—those pictures—not really—"

"Not the pictures. The picture. Just one of them. From it I deduce, among other things, that if you go back to that house you're apt to get killed. And you're certainly going to be needed, so—Yes, Fritz?"

Fritz, having closed the door behind him, advanced halfway to the desk and spoke:

"A caller, sir. Mr. John Charles Dunn. A gentleman and three ladies are with him."

Chapter 16

There was an instant's silence and then Sara Dunn popped out of her chair and pretended she was a cyclone.

At that, she was young and active, and might have presented difficulties if her hands had been free to continue with my face where Daisy had left off the day before, but she was using them to collect snapshots. She had the envelope containing the film and the discards in one hand, and was reaching for the remaining six with the other, when I gathered her in. I did it promptly and neatly, with my left arm clamping both her arms and her body above the waist, and my right hand smothering her mouth and nose and pushing the back of her head into my ribs. She couldn't even kick, because my knees had her legs pinned against the desk.

Wolfe asked, "Are you hurting her?"

"Not to speak of."

He grunted, got up and came around the desk, and retrieved the envelope from her left hand. There wasn't much grip in her fingers on account of the pressure on her arm. Then he collected the six pictures she hadn't got hold of, dropped them into the envelope, crossed to the safe, put the envelope in a drawer, and closed the safe door.

He ambled back to his chair and deposited himself, and told me with a frown, "I don't like the look on your face when you're doing things like that. Turn her loose."

"She may scream."

"Then hold on a minute." He directed his eyes at hers. "You have done everything you can, and it cannot be undone. I'm going to finish this business as soon as possible. None of your family—your father and mother and brother—will suffer by it, nor will you. But I don't want any talk about those pictures. Furthermore, you are not to leave this house. The attempt to steal that film shows that the murderer is aware of the blunder he made. He doesn't know where the pictures are and I don't want him to know just yet, but he knows that anything seen by your camera was seen by you too. He's a bungler and an ass, but that merely increases your danger. Unless you promise not to leave this house, I'll have to feed the police a lot of stuff they're not prepared to digest, to let them take the responsibility for your death instead of me—Let her go, Archie."

She was half Hawthorne and there was no telling about her reactions, so I unwrapped my arms and retreated two paces simultaneously. But she ignored me completely. She straightened up there against the desk, inhaled with a couple of gasps to catch up on her oxygen, and sputtered at Wolfe:

"You said *he*."

Wolfe shook his head. "You'll have to wait, Miss Dunn. It will be ticklish going. I'm paying you a compliment by not having Mr. Goodwin tape your mouth shut and lock you in upstairs. I'm going by your eyes. You're not to leave this house, and you're to tell no one about those pictures—"

The door burst open and John Charles Dunn stumbled in, with May and June, Celia Fleet, and Osric Stauffer at his heels. He didn't literally stumble, but he did run into a chair, and then stopped and grabbed the back of it and stood there and said:

"I got tired waiting. We got tired waiting."

Sara looked at him, at his sagging face and bloodshot eyes, and then made a dive for him, crying out, "Daddy! Daddy dear!"

She put her arms around his neck and kissed him. Apparently the professional fiend acting that way served to release tension all around. Dunn put his arm around his daughter's shoulders and made noises in his throat. Celia Fleet stared at them and chewed on her lower lip. Stauffer glared around with eyes as bloodshot as Dunn's. June sat down and got out her handkerchief and wiped off two tears that had started down her cheeks. May marched up to the desk and said to Wolfe in a biting and contemptuous tone:

"I didn't want to come here. My sister and brother-in-law insisted on it. Which was it, funk or treachery?"

"Now, Miss Hawthorne—" Stauffer approached remonstrating, "That won't help the situation—"

"April's arrested," June blurted. "They've arrested her!"

I was trying to help out by pushing chairs behind

knees here and there. They certainly were a woe-
begone outfit.

"She's not arrested," Dunn said as he sank into a
chair without looking at it. Still a lawyer, in misfor-
tune up to his chin. "She was asked to go to the district
attorney's office and she went. But the way it stands
now—"

"I tell you, John," May snapped at him, "before we
tell this man anything, we should demand a satisfactory explanation—"

"Nonsense," Stauffer sputtered irritably. "Damn it
all, you talk as if we could choose—"

"Please, all of you!" Wolfe pushed air with his
palm. "Stop jabbering. Your minds aren't working."
He looked at May. "Apparently, Miss Hawthorne, you
are resentful because when we found Miss Karn's dead
body I came home to think it over instead of sitting
there all night starving and twiddling my thumbs. I
thought you had more sense. To answer your question, it was neither funk nor treachery; it was wit.
Anyhow, I'm not answerable to you. You, with others,
engaged me to negotiate with Miss Karn, but Miss
Karn is dead. Mr. Dunn engaged me to investigate the
murder of Noel Hawthorne." He looked at Dunn. "Am
I still so engaged?"

"Yes. Of course." Dunn didn't sound very enthusiastic. "But I don't know what you can do—Prescott's
down there with April—"

"Let's clear the air a little," Wolfe suggested.
"April is in no danger whatever, except of being
annoyed."

They all stared at him. May demanded, "How do
you know that?"

"I know more than that," Wolfe assured her. "But that's what I give you now. Accept it; it's good— Next, Mr. Dunn, I offer you a suggestion. Yesterday Mr. Goodwin found Miss Karn seated in the living room, talking with April Hawthorne who was disguised with a veil to pass as Mrs. Noel Hawthorne."

Dunn nodded. "That was one thing—"

"One thing you came here now to see me about. Of course. But my suggestion: Mr. Goodwin, on an impulse, parted the draperies that conceal the bar, and saw Mr. Stauffer standing there. Last evening Stauffer offered Goodwin a thousand dollars not to tell the police about it. Goodwin refused the bribe, but he didn't tell the police, and I didn't tell Inspector Cramer when he called on me this morning. But we might strike a bargain with Stauffer. Since he was Hawthorne's deputy in the foreign department of Daniel Cullen and Company, he must know the truth about that leakage on the Argentine loan. If it happened as you suspected yesterday, when Mrs. Hawthorne was found—"

"You're way behind," Stauffer interrupted gruffly.

Wolfe's brow lifted. "Behind?"

"Yes. You're going to suggest that Dunn forces me to tell the truth about the loan business by threatening to inform the police that I was hiding behind that curtain when Naomi Karn was there. Aren't you?"

"I thought we might try that."

"Well, you're late. As long as Hawthorne was alive it was impossible for me to tell Dunn about it, I simply couldn't, but I told him this morning, and we confronted Mrs. Hawthorne with it and made her sign a

statement. That was what made her vindictive enough
to go to the police with a bunch of lies—"

"We don't know that she lied," May objected.
"Even if she stuck to the truth, it's enough to challenge Wolfe's statement that April's in no danger—"

"Let's clean up as we go along," Wolfe put in. "Then
you're clear on the affair of the loan, Mr. Dunn?"

"I'm clear of perfidy," Dunn said gloomily, "but I
let that damned woman make a fool of me. And
anyway, with all this—it's all over—"

"Not quite," Wolfe declared. "It won't be all over
until I'm through with it. With luck even, you should
be able to sleep tonight, or tomorrow at the latest. But
you can help me remove a few obstructions—excuse
me—"

The phone was ringing. I got my receiver at my
ear, but he must have been on edge, for he reached for
his extension without waiting for me. I said, "Office of
Nero Wolfe—"

"Saul Panzer, Archie. Three-eighteen. I'm report-
ing from—"

Wolfe's voice cut him off: "Hold the wire." Wolfe
dropped his instrument on its cradle, arose from his
chair, said curtly, "No record, Archie," and made for
the door. Fritz, who had been hovering, left the room
with him. I plugged in the kitchen extension, kept the
receiver to my ear until I heard Wolfe's voice and
Saul's answering him, and hung up.

May Hawthorne said incisively, "He's a mounte-
bank. Talk of our sleeping tonight! I tell you, someone
must do something! Prescott down there with April!
He may be a good lawyer, but he's not up to this. And

Andy's a child. And this windbag of a Wolfe—bah! We're sunk, damn it!"

Dunn muttered at her, without conviction, "He says April is in no danger—"

"Bluff!" May snorted. "My God, if the best we can do in the face of calamity is sit here and listen—"

"Be quiet, May," June put in with quiet authority. "Quit ragging. You know very well it's Nero Wolfe or nothing. What has anyone else been able to offer except well-meaning condolence? If we're sunk, we're sunk. You stop digging at John. He was on the verge of a collapse before this happened." Her eyes left her sister, to look at her daughter, and her voice changed. "Sara dear. I don't like to ask you what you came here for, but I'd like to know. Mr. Wolfe sent for you. Didn't he?"

"Yes." Sara was on a chair next to her father. "He wanted to ask me something. About my camera being stolen. You remember I spoke about it yesterday, and last evening I told Mr. Goodwin. Of course that was all I could tell Mr. Wolfe, that it was gone and I had no idea who took it."

So they discussed the camera. There had been two murders, an estate of millions had apparently gone up the flue as far as they were concerned, Dunn was tumbling headlong off of a national eminence, their April was being questioned by the police as a suspect, and they discussed the camera. That would have been all right if they had had any idea of its relation to the cataclysm, but as far as I could tell nobody had. They were still discussing it when Wolfe came back in.

He got into his chair and looked around at the faces. "Now," he said brusquely, "let's tidy up a little.

First, Mrs. Hawthorne's vindictiveness after you cornered her on that loan business. I suppose one of the things she told the police was about the cornflower Andy found hanging on a briar, and April's wearing a bunch of cornflowers Tuesday afternoon which had been presented to her by Mr. Stauffer."

There were stares and two or three exclamations. Stauffer started, "How the devil—"

Wolfe wiggled a finger. "Let me go on. I'm not trying to stagger you with effects. I got that story firsthand, from Mrs. Hawthorne herself yesterday. Did she give it to the police?"

"Yes, she did," June replied.

"Describing, of course, the scene she saw through a window Tuesday evening, when Andy exhibited the cornflower to you and your husband and told where he had found it. I suppose the police questioned you about that?"

"Yes."

"Did you admit it?"

"Of course not. It wasn't true. We denied it."

"All three of you?"

"Yes."

Wolfe grunted. "That's bad. You're going to regret that."

"Why should we regret it, since we merely—"

"Merely told the truth, Mrs. Dunn? Oh, no. You lied. Don't take me for a fool. You shouldn't even take Mr. Cramer for a fool. Mrs. Hawthorne didn't invent that story. The fact is, you should have told me about it yourself, since you were hiring me for this job. And you'll tell me the truth now, or you'll get out of my office and take the job with you. I'm not being high-handed just for the devil of it. It's important, it may even be vital, that I have a statement from you, your husband and your son, that that cornflower was found there and all three of you saw it. Well?"

"It's a trick," May snapped.

"Pfui!" Wolfe made a face at her. "This thing is turning you into a dunce. I don't play tricks on clients." He looked at June. "Well?"

Dunn demanded, "Do you have any basis for your assertion that April is not in danger?"

"I do. I'm not disclosing it, but I have it. You'd better either acquire some confidence in me, sir, or fire me."

"All right. Andy found a cornflower there and showed it to my wife and me."

"Tuesday evening, as Mrs. Hawthorne said?"

"Yes."

"What did you do with it?"

"I threw it in the fireplace."

"Do you confirm that, Mrs. Dunn?"

June hesitated a second and then said firmly, "Yes."

"Good." Wolfe frowned at her. "You'll have to eat your denial to the police, but that's your fault. You had hired me and you should have consulted me. Next. Your sister's masquerade as Mrs. Hawthorne. Mr. Goodwin saw her there with Miss Karn, came straight to the library, and saw Mrs. Hawthorne with me. He ascertained that the one in the library was the real Mrs. Hawthorne by trying to lift her veil. You heard her scream. We concluded that the counterfeit downstairs must be April, the accomplished actress. Did Mrs. Hawthorne give that to the police too?"

"Yes," June replied.

"How did she know about it?"

"Turner told her. The butler. I happened to be in the entrance hall when Miss Karn arrived and said she wanted to see Mrs. Hawthorne. I told Turner to put Miss Karn in the living room and I would attend to it. On my way upstairs I had an idea. Daisy was in the library with you. The idea was for April to get a dress and veil from Daisy's room and see Miss Karn and find out what she had to say. I found her in May's room and suggested it, and they approved. Mr. Stauffer was there too, and he—"

"I didn't," Stauffer put in curtly. "I mean I didn't approve. I strongly disapproved. I went down and entered the bar from the rear and stayed there behind the curtain as a protection for April. Goodwin saw me there."

"And Turner?" Wolfe asked June.

"I don't think he suspected anything when he saw April come downstairs. She was perfect. She always is. But he knew Daisy was in the library at a moment when she was also in the living room, for he saw her there when he went to tell you that one of your men had arrived. He couldn't tell his mistress about it at once, for he didn't know which one was her, but he told her later."

"And now she has told the police."

"Yes."

"And you have all been questioned."

"Yes."

"And you have, I hope—except Mr. Stauffer—told it just as it happened."

"Of course not. We denied it."

"Good heavens." Wolfe sighed and compressed his lips. "You have denied the whole thing?"

"Yes."

"April too?"

"Yes."

"And Turner presumably is a mealymouthed liar?"

"No. He must—we merely said—he must be mistaken."

"God bless you." Wolfe was disgusted. "He'd better. You merely said! It's a wonder you're not all locked up! Was Prescott in on this?"

"No. No one knew of it except April and May and me—and Mr. Stauffer. Not even my husband, until this morning." June fluttered a hand at him. "And I appeal to you, Mr. Wolfe, to—to understand. Ordinarily I'm not a fool, none of us is. But we've been so shocked and bewildered and helpless—all the sense we had was knocked out of us. For my husband and me this came at the end of months of frightful strain— you must understand—"

She faltered to a stop. Wolfe said gruffly, "My understanding wouldn't help you any. You can get that anywhere. Tell me what Miss Karn said to your sister disguised as Mrs. Hawthorne."

"She wanted a million dollars."

"You mean she offered to sign over all but a million?"

"Yes. She said the offer you had made her was ridiculous, but she would be satisfied with a million. April left soon after Mr. Goodwin saw her there, because she knew he would see Daisy in the library. She told Miss Karn she was going upstairs to consult

with us about her offer, but she went straight to
Daisy's room and got rid of the dress and veil."

"And you, Mr. Stauffer? How long did you stay
behind the curtain?"

"I stayed a while because I thought April might
come back. Then when Goodwin looked in and saw me,
I realized that she wouldn't. I left a few seconds after
that, by the rear."

"Miss Karn was there sitting on a chair when you
left?"

"I suppose she was. I didn't see her."

Wolfe's gaze swept the faces. "Here's a question for
all of you. When Mr. Goodwin left the living room
after a brief conversation with Miss Karn, it was ten
minutes past three. Has anyone admitted seeing her
there, alive, after that?"

They all shook their heads. Dunn said, "Prescott tells
me that Davis said Miss Karn was not in the living room
when he entered it a little before five o'clock."

"Did Turner take Davis to the living room?"

"No. They let me read Turner's statement. Davis
entered the living room alone and Turner went upstairs to find Prescott."

"Does Davis admit that?"

"He hasn't admitted anything. They can't find him.
At least they hadn't found him at noon today."

"Indeed." Wolfe's eyes half closed. "Do you know
where he is?"

"Of course not. How could I?"

"I don't know, I'm asking. I should think Prescott
might know. Davis bolted out of the library yesterday
at a quarter to six, and Prescott went after him a
moment later. What about that?"

"Prescott says he reached the entrance hall just as Davis was opening the front door to leave. He called to him, but Davis went on out without answering. Turner was there and his statement verifies that. Stauffer and I were in the living room with that police lieutenant and Ritchie of the Cosmopolitan Trust. I myself heard Prescott's voice calling Davis's name, and went to the hall and asked him to join us in the living room. A few minutes later we sent Turner upstairs to ask you to come down." Dunn's voice was better, and a gleam of life, even intelligence, was showing itself in his eyes. He fixed them on Wolfe, calculating, and suddenly demanded, "What about Davis?"

Wolfe shook his head. "Nothing much. Curiosity. The fact that he can't be found—"

"I don't believe it." Dunn's voice was getting obstreperous. "Your man was telling you something about Davis yesterday—about finding him somewhere drunk. If you expect me to have confidence in you, at least you can give me an idea of what—"

"No, I can't!" Wolfe cut him off. "What good will an idea do you? I'll give you something much better than an idea, as soon as I can, and I'll let you know when it's ready. You ought to eat something." He looked around. "All of you. Eat something and take off your shoes and lie down a while."

"My Lord," May Hawthorne said. "If you're a humbug you're a good one. It's four o'clock and you're going upstairs to your orchids."

"I am," Wolfe agreed. "And arrange a few things, including my mind." He arose, and looked at Sara. "If you'll come with me, Miss Dunn? You said you'd like to."

Chapter 17

When Inspector Cramer arrived, a little before six o'clock, I was in the kitchen squeezing lemons. Various things had happened during the hundred minutes since Wolfe had gone off upstairs with Sara Dunn, approximately in this order:

The visitors had departed, not much less downhearted than when they arrived, after informing us that they had checked out of the Hawthorne mansion on 67th Street and moved to a hotel. Daisy's chumminess with the police accounted for that.

Wolfe had phoned some orders down from the roof. To send Orrie Cather up to him for instructions was the first one. I had done so, and a little later Orrie had come down and left the house. Second, to send Fred Durkin to the address on 11th Street where Eugene Davis was Earl Dawson, with instructions to get him and bring him to the office. I instructed Fred and dispatched him. Third, to get Raymond Plehn on the phone if possible. That one was entirely beyond me. Plehn was the horticultural expert of Ditson and Company, the big wholesale florists. It was still be-

yond me after I got him, and listened in, and heard
Wolfe ask him to come down to the house as soon as
possible.

Saul Panzer and Johnny Keems both phoned in,
and in both cases Wolfe told me to connect them
upstairs and no record was needed, which meant that
my powers of dissimulation were not to be subjected
to an undue strain, and it didn't help my temper any
that I didn't even know for whose benefit the dissem-
bling would have been necessary.

Another thing that failed to soothe my temper was
the fact that I indulged in a private session of "What's
Wrong with this Picture?" and it didn't get me anywhere. I got the six snapshots from the safe and took
them to a window and studied them with the big glass
in the strong light, and as far as solving a murder was
concerned I might as well have been studying picture
post cards from the Grand Canyon. If it was there, it
wasn't there for me; but I was going on with it when
Raymond Plehn arrived. I announced him, and Wolfe
told me to have Fritz take him up in the elevator,
together with the envelope of snapshots, the magnifying glass, and the thing in the vase in the kitchen
which Fred had brought back from Rockland County
with his bag of clues. That put me in a first-class
mood. I knew it was on the level, for he wouldn't have
got Plehn down there just to make me itch, but I
paced the office floor and concentrated on it and
couldn't even get within a mile of a wild guess. I was
still stabbing around at it when I heard the elevator
descending and Fritz leading Plehn out at the front
door. He came to the office to give me the envelope,

which I returned to the drawer in the safe without any further attempt at homework.

Meanwhile there had been two more phone calls. John Charles Dunn first, from his hotel room, to say that April had got back from the district attorney's office safe and sound, with nothing worse than a bad headache, and that Andy Dunn had returned with her but not Prescott. Prescott had remained with them throughout the interview, but then had left them, sending a message to Dunn that he would communicate with him later. The second call was from Fred Durkin. He reported that he had rung the bell marked "Dawson" and got no response, had got admitted by the janitor and gone up to the apartment, and had found the door locked and got no reply to knocks or kicks. He was phoning from a drugstore around the corner. I told him to hold the wire, rang Wolfe on the house line, and relayed instructions to Fred to camp.

Shortly after that, while I was in the kitchen squeezing lemons, Cramer arrived. Fritz put him in the office, and pretty soon I joined him there and offered him a glass of good cold lemonade. He wouldn't even say no, he merely growled. From the dirty look he gave me, you might have thought I had written to the mayor about him.

I put both glasses on my desk, sat down and told him, "This weather is simply frightful," and stirred with a spoon.

"To hell with you," he observed. "I want to see Wolfe."

"Okay, brother." I sipped lemonade. "He'll be down in a few minutes. Nothing you say to him will hurt my feelings any. I intend to resign. He's being crafty and mysterious again, and I'm fed up with it. You know? People phoning in by the dozen, and I mustn't listen because I can't keep my face straight. Phooey. What I am, I'm a helot. A damn flunky. How's chances for a job on the force?"

"Shut up."

"All right, I'll surprise you. I'll shut up." I did so, and drank lemonade. I had finished the first glass and was starting on the second when Wolfe entered. Apparently he had left Sara up with Theodore Horstmann, for he was alone. He greeted Cramer, got seated behind his desk, rang for beer, and heaved a sigh.

He regarded the inspector with his eyes nearly shut. "Something new?"

"No." Cramer's voice wasn't pleasant. "Something old." He pulled a piece of paper from his pocket, unfolded it and glanced at it, and slid it across the desk. "Take a look at that."

Wolfe picked it up, glanced over it, let it fall to the desk, and leaned back again. A little noise came from him, something between a gurgle and a chuckle. "That thing's dated today," he declared. "I wouldn't call that old."

"No." Cramer agreed, "that part of it's fresh enough. But what made it necessary—your same old tricks. You've got no kick coming. I offered you an open road this morning, and you wouldn't take it. Okay, I'm doing you a favor by coming after you myself. You've done it once too often. Even if I was inclined to play tag with you, I couldn't. Everybody from the President of the United States down to the president of the senior class at Varney College is trying to horn in. I swear to God. But I'm not apologizing." He turned a thumb to point it at the paper on the desk. "Skinner suggested that, but I didn't oppose it. I've warned you fifty times you'd fall in some day, and this is it. What the hell did you think, because your clients are people of position and power and influence you could depend on them to pull you out, no matter—"

"I don't depend on my clients. They depend on me."

"Well, they're out of luck this time. I gave you plenty of chance this morning. A chance to spill what Mrs. Hawthorne told you about young Dunn finding that cornflower. A chance to come clean about April Hawthorne's being there with Naomi Karn disguised with a veil. Just to show you there's no out on that, we know that Goodwin saw her there and three seconds later saw Mrs. Hawthorne in the library with you. It's things like those we're going to discuss downtown, those and a few others. Come on, get your hat. I've got a car outside that don't jolt much."

Wolfe looked mildly incredulous, and spoke mildly. "Nonsense. Tell me what you want."

"I told you this morning, and what good did it do me?" Cramer arose. "Come on, they're waiting for us down at Skinner's office."

"Today is Sunday, Mr. Cramer."

"Correct. I doubt if you can get bail before tomorrow. We'll find a cot big enough for you."

"You haven't got one. This is grotesque."

"Sure it is. Come on. I may get tired of being polite."

"You mean this. Do you?"

"I do, you know."

"Then I request a courtesy. I want three or four minutes to dictate a letter. In your presence."

Cramer scowled at him suspiciously. "Who to?"

"You'll hear it."

Cramer hesitated a moment, sat down, and growled, "Go ahead."

Wolfe said, "Your notebook, Archie." I opened the drawer and got it out. He leaned back and closed his eyes and started off in his usual smooth monotone:

"To W. B. Oliver, Editor of the *Gazette*. Dear Mr. Oliver. Inspector Fergus Cramer has arrested me as a material witness in the Hawthorne-Karn murder case, and I may be unable to get out on bail before morning. I therefore wish to expose him and his superiors to ridicule and derision, and luckily am in a position to do so. You know whether my word may be relied upon. I suggest that you publish these facts in your Monday city edition: That my arrest was motivated by professional pique. That by my own brilliant and ingenious interpretation of evidence, I have discovered the identity of the murderer. That I am not prepared as yet to disclose the murderer's identity to the police, for fear their bungling—hint at worse if you care to—will prematurely spring a trap I have set for the criminal. That when the time comes—you may say soon—the arrest will be made by representatives of the *Gazette*, and the murderer will be delivered by them to the police, together with conclusive evidence of guilt. I shall certainly be out on bail by Monday noon at the latest, and if you will kindly come to my house at 1:30 for lunch, we can discuss details, including the sum your paper will be willing to pay for this coup. With the best wishes and regards, cordially

yours. Sign my name and make sure it reaches Mr.
Oliver before ten o'clock tonight."

Wolfe got to his feet, grunting as usual. "Well, sir.
I'm ready."

Cramer, not stirring, growled, "Oliver won't get
that. I take Goodwin too."

Wolfe shrugged. "That would delay it twenty-four
hours. He would publish Tuesday instead of Monday."

"He wouldn't dare. Neither would you. You know
the law. Oliver wouldn't dare touch it. This case—"

"Bah. No matter what the law is, if we deliver the
murderer and the evidence we'll be heroes. I'm ready
to go."

"You'll lose your license."

"I'll collect enough from the *Gazette* to retire on."

"How much of that is bluff?"

"None of it. I'm giving Mr. Oliver my word."

Cramer glared at me. I grinned at him sympathetically. He cocked his head at Wolfe, and suddenly
acquired an excess of blood above the neck and made
an exhibition of himself. He jerked up, slammed the
desk with his fist, and yelled at Wolfe. "Sit down! You
goddamn rhinoceros! Sit down!"

The phone rang.

I swiveled and got it, spoke to it, and heard Fred
Durkin's voice, low, husky and urgent:

"Archie? Come up here as quick as you can! I'm in
that place again, and I've got a corpse or he soon will
be!"

"I'm sorry," I said politely, "but I haven't had a
chance to speak to Mr. Wolfe about it. I'm sure he can't
come now—he's engaged here with a visitor from the
police—hold the wire, please." I addressed Wolfe,

with the receiver close enough so Fred would get it too: "This is that fellow Dawson. He phoned this afternoon. He's got a crate of Cattleya Mossiae from Venezuela, and he wants a hundred bucks for a dozen. He's had an offer—"

"I can't go now."

"I know you can't—"

"But you can. Tell him you'll be there right away."

I spoke to the phone: "Mr. Wolfe says he wants them if they're in good condition, Mr. Dawson. I'll come and take a look at them. You can expect me in fifteen minutes."

I hung up and marched out. One of the things I didn't like about it was that if Cramer decided to get suspicious it would be a cinch for him to step to the phone and have the call traced, but by the look on his face I judged that his mind was occupied with other affairs.

At the curb in front, Cramer's car was nosing the roadster's tail. I nodded a cheerful greeting to the two dicks on the driver's seat, hopped in the roadster, and rolled. It wasn't likely that they had any instructions that would cause them to follow me, but I made sure by circling into 34th Street and halting for a couple of minutes, and then headed downtown. At that time of a July Sunday afternoon the streets were nearly deserted, and I had only a little more than a mile to go. I parked where I had the day before, a little distance east of the address, trotted to the vestibule and pushed the button under Dawson, opened the door when I heard the click, and mounted the two flights.

At the door at the end of the hall, which was halfway open, I was confronted by two evidences of violence. A panel of the door and part of its frame was in splinters. That was one. The other was Fred Durkin's face. The left side of his jaw was swollen, and there was a bruise on his right temple with the skin raw.

"Oh," I said. "You're the corpse, huh?"

"Huh yourself," he retorted with Irish wit. "Look at this." I followed him inside, and saw more evidences of violence. A table and a chair had been overturned and a couple of rugs were messed up, and lying there on the floor was Glenn Prescott. His eyes were open, staring up at us. His face was in much worse shape than Fred's, and there was blood here and there, mostly on his collar and tie and the front of his shirt.

"He came to," Fred said, "but he won't talk. I wiped some blood off his face, but it dribbles out of his nose."

Prescott let out a moan. "I'll—talk," he mumbled thickly. "I'll talk if—I can. I'm afraid I'm hurt— internally." His hand groped around his belly. "He hit me there."

I knelt beside him and felt his pulse. Then I started feeling and poking all around. He winced and said ouch and moaned, but I couldn't find any indication of agony. Fred brought me a wet towel and I cleaned his face off some.

I stood up. "I don't think you're hurt much, but of course I'm not sure. He didn't hit you with anything but his fists, did he?"

"I don't know. He knocked me down—and I got up—and he knocked me down again—"

"Who was it, Davis?"

"I'm not going—" He moaned.

"Sure it was Davis," Fred put in. "He must have come while I was around the corner phoning you. I came back and watched the entrance, and pretty soon this guy walked up and pushed the button and went in. After a while I heard noises. The janitor came out from below and said he heard them too. He let me in, but he said he wasn't looking for trouble and didn't come up with me. Just as I got to the top of the second flight I got it. I caught a glimpse of him, but not quick enough. My head musta hit on the corner. When I come to I was wedged in there at the turn of the stairs, and he was gone. I came up and busted in the door and here was this guy on the floor."

I looked around, saw the phone, went to it, and dialed a number. In a minute Wolfe's voice answered.

"Archie," I told him. "Is Cramer still there?"

"Yes."

"Do I report?"

"Yes."

"I'm talking from Dawson's apartment. Prescott is here on the floor bruised up a little. Davis played tunes on him and knocked Fred downstairs and went out for a walk. Fred's here."

"Is Prescott badly hurt?"

"I don't think so."

"Bring him here."

"What about Cramer? His car's out front with two dicks."

"That's all right. We are co-operating with the police."

"Oh. Goody."

I hung up and turned to Prescott. "Inspector Cramer is in Nero Wolfe's office and wants to see you.

We're going to put you on your feet and help you downstairs."

He moaned. "But I may be injured—it may be dangerous—"

"I don't think so. We'll see if you can stand up. Here, Fred."

We got him erect without anything breaking. From the way he groaned you might have thought he wasn't worth bothering with, but after we stood him up I tried his pulse and it was as good as mine. So we walked him and let him groan. When we got him down to the ground floor we sat him on a step and I went out and moved the roadster to the curb in front. Then we took him out and hoisted him in, and I climbed in behind the wheel and told Fred to hop in the rumble seat.

Fred, standing on the sidewalk, shook his head. "You don't need me. I got an errand."

"They'll want to ask you. Get in."

"They can ask me later. I got a certain matter."

I looked at him. There was an edge to his voice, and a glint in his eye, that showed me there was no use arguing.

"All right," I said, "there's one chance in a million you might find him there. If you do, don't be a sap. Remember that any citizen who sees a crime committed, like for instance assault and battery, can legally make an arrest. You may not have seen it much, but you sure felt it."

"Go float on a rock," he said, and tramped off. I saw that Prescott was propped in his corner, and started the car.

On the way up to 35th Street, Prescott put his

hand on my arm and said he had decided he had better
go to a hospital. I didn't bother to persuade him out of
it, but just kept going. In front of Wolfe's house, the
two city employees in Cramer's car were obviously
expecting us. They helped me ease my cargo out to the
sidewalk, paying no more attention to his protests
than I did as we took him up the stoop and on inside.
In the hall we were met not only by Wolfe and
Cramer, but also by Doc Vollmer, whose office was up
the street. Wolfe took command and gave the instructions. The doctor and one of the dicks walked upstairs
while I ascended with Prescott in the elevator. I left
him there with them in the south bedroom, the spare
on the same floor as mine, and went back down to the
office.

Wolfe and Cramer were sitting there. I made my
report, though there wasn't a lot to add to what I had
told Wolfe on the phone. Wolfe held himself in, but I
could tell by the look of his eyes that it was only the
presence of company that restrained him from making
pointed remarks about Fred Durkin. I gathered that
the person who was really wanted to make it a good
party was Mr. Eugene Davis. Cramer got his office on
the phone, and from the orders he barked to some
underling it was evident that Wolfe had told him all
about the Davis-Dawson angle and that every cop on
the force was already searching for the junior partner
of the dear old firm.

Just as Cramer hung up, the doorbell started
buzzing and didn't stop. I beat it for the hall, bumped
into Fritz, and told him I would tend to it. I swung the
door wide, and after one glance stepped aside with a
welcoming grin. The extra dick was standing on the

second step, looking alert but uncertain, staring up. Confronting me was Eugene-Earl-Davis-Dawson, haggard, untidy, without a hat, and at his elbow, with a gun stuck against his ribs, was Fred Durkin.

"Well, well," I observed approvingly.

Fred, intent on his errand, disregarded me. "March, you big ape," he commanded, prodding with the gun, and Davis marched. I shut the door and followed them into the office. Fred kept him going right up to Wolfe's desk, and then dropped the gun in his pocket and faced his captive.

"Take a run," he said grimly. "Or make a pass at me or something. All I ask—"

"That will do, Fred," said Wolfe curtly. "Where did you find him?"

"At Wellman's. A joint on 8th Street. The place where—"

"Very well. Satisfactory. Is he armed?"

"No, sir."

"Good. Sit down, Mr. Davis. It looks as if—"

The door opened and Doc Vollmer entered. He saw the tableau, halted, and then approached. "Excuse me, but I have to run. Patients waiting. That man upstairs will be all right. He's got some bruises, but that's all except that his nerves are in extremely bad condition. I advise a sedative."

"Thank you, doctor. We'll attend to the sedative. Run along." Wolfe looked at Davis. "It's Mr. Prescott. We brought him here. It's amazing that you didn't kill him, really amazing." He looked at the inspector. "I believe we can go ahead now, Mr. Cramer, only it would be best to have Mr. Dunn here. All of them, I suppose. If you will please phone his hotel?"

Chapter 18

I n the south bedroom, a hot south wind fluttered the curtains at the windows. The dick put on his coat, wiped his face and neck with his handkerchief, and smoothed his hair back with his hands. Glenn Prescott sat on a chair and groaned.

"I'm perfectly willing to talk to Wolfe," he said in a hurt tone. "But why can't he come up here? I can't even bend over to put my shoes on."

Having got him off of the bed and his clothes more or less arranged on him, I was tired of fooling with him. I got a shoe horn from the dresser, went over and kneeled down by him, got him shod and the strings tied, stood up and told him:

"One, two, three, go. For God's sake, do you want us to carry you?"

The dick said irritably, "There's an elevator ain't they? What more do you want?"

Prescott gritted his teeth, pushed himself upright with his hands, groaned, and took a step.

Downstairs, just inside the door of the office, he stopped short, evidently surprised at the size of the party. The room was full, extra chairs having been brought from the front. Sara Dunn had come down from the roof and was in the corner of the bookshelves with Andy and Celia. Wolfe was at his desk and Cramer and District Attorney Skinner were at the far end of it, with Eugene Davis between them. April, May and June, between us and the desk, had their backs to us as we entered. Stauffer was on a chair next to April's, still protecting her. John Charles Dunn got up and approached, starting at Prescott's face.

"Glenn! What happened to you? Good heavens, what—"

Prescott vaguely shook his head. I doubt if he heard Dunn or even saw him. His eyes, one of them puffed half shut, were aimed straight past him, in the direction of Eugene Davis. He stood there, with me behind him. The dick had posted himself at the door.

Skinner barked, "Well?"

Wolfe said, "There's a chair for Mr. Prescott there by yours, Archie."

I nudged Prescott's elbow and he moved across to it and lowered himself. Johnny Keems got out of my chair and moved to one in the rear alongside Saul Panzer. He knew damn well I didn't like anyone sitting in my chair.

May Hawthorne said sarcastically, "This is impressive, Mr. Wolfe."

Wolfe's eyes moved to her. "You don't like me, do you, Miss Hawthorne? I understand that. You're a realist and I'm a romantic. But all this isn't for effect. I shall need some of you and I may need all of you. It's a job. I'm out after a murderer and he's here." He looked at the district attorney. "It may be slippery going, Mr. Skinner. I expect you to stick to our bargain."

"As stated," said Skinner sharply. "I'm not gagged and I won't be."

"Yes, sir, as stated." Wolfe's eyes circled around the faces and settled on the one least presentable of all. "Mr. Prescott, I know you can't talk without discomfort, so I'll try to do most of it myself. Being a lawyer, you understand of course that you are under no compulsion to answer questions, but I warn you I'm going to be pretty stubborn and disagreeable. First I'll ask you to verify a few facts I've collected. In March, 1938, your private secretary was a young woman named—what's that name, Saul?"

Saul spoke up from the rear: "Lucille Adams."

"And when did she die?"

"Two months ago, in May, of tuberculosis, at her home at 2419—"

"Thanks. Is that correct, Mr. Prescott?"

"Why—yes," Prescott mumbled.

"It was Miss Adams to whom you dictated Noel Hawthorne's will, following instructions he gave you?"

"I don't remember." The mumble cleared up a little. "I suppose it was."

"She was your private secretary at that time, and took all your confidential dictation?"

"Yes."

A voice said gruffly, "If this is a joke it's a bad one." It was Eugene Davis. "Is this an official investigation? The district attorney is here. Are you on his staff, Mr. Wolfe?"

"No, sir. I'm a private detective—Are you represented by counsel, Mr. Prescott? Or do you want to be?"

"Certainly not."

"Do you want Mr. Davis, as your counsel, interfering in our conversation?"

"No."

"Then to go on. Regarding the routine in your office. The notebooks used by the confidential secretaries are numbered. As soon as one is filled and the contents transcribed, the notebooks are turned in and destroyed. Is that correct?"

Prescott carefully shifted in his chair, but he didn't groan. "Yes," he said. "I'm answering the question, yes. Now I'd like to ask one. I'd like to know who has been investigating the affairs of my office, and why."

"I have." Wolfe's tone got a little crisper. "My agents have. Mr. Panzer and Mr. Keems, there behind you. I assure you they have done nothing actionable, and if you start pumping up indignation it will only rush blood to your head and make you more uncomfortable than you already are. You'd better keep your brain as cool as possible."

"Get on with it," the district attorney snapped. "We're not here for a lecture."

Wolfe didn't even glance at him. He continued at Prescott: "Now, sir, if Mr. Skinner will stop interrupting me, I can make it pretty brief. I have been given, one after the other, three problems to solve: the will of Noel Hawthorne, the murder of Noel Hawthorne, and the murder of Naomi Karn. Whether my belief that I have solved them is sound, or whether it is merely my conceit bubbling over, rests on the validity of a series of hypotheses I have made—based, of course, on information received. If any one of them is wrong, I am wrong. I'm going to ask you—all of you—to listen closely to them.

"One. Eugene Davis was madly, desperately, in love with Naomi Karn, and was so filled with despair and jealousy when she abandoned him for Noel Hawthorne that he began drinking too much and, I suppose, did other foolish things. That went on for nearly three years. During that time, possibly, she let him have some crumbs—did she, Mr. Davis? It would help to understand her character."

All eyes went to Davis. He made no answer. With his lips tight and his jaw locked, he gazed at Wolfe. A spasm contorted the muscles of his throat as he swallowed.

Wolfe shrugged. "Two. Davis understood Miss Karn's character himself. He knew she was ambitious, greedy, and unscrupulous, and that he would never find relief from the agony he suffered through her intimacy with Noel Hawthorne as long as Hawthorne was alive and a millionaire. Also he knew the terms of Hawthorne's will. It was in the vault of his firm, to which he had access.

"Three. Probably the death of Lucille Adams, two months ago, led to the formation of his scheme. A shrewd brain sees an opportunity where an ordinary one would miss it. Anyway, he made his scheme, and awaited an occasion to execute it. He knew of Hawthorne's intended trip to Rockland County for Tuesday afternoon, and arranged to be with Miss Karn at that time. He says they drove to Connecticut; wherever they went, he absented himself long enough to go to Rockland County and back. Probably he had a detailed plan of action, and a weapon; but seeing, from the highway, Noel Hawthorne there at the edge of the woods carrying a shotgun, was a heaven-sent opportunity. He took advantage of it. I'm pretty sure Miss Karn didn't know where he was or what he was doing. She didn't need to, and he didn't want her to.

"Four. Tuesday evening—"

"Wait a minute." Eugene Davis had decided it was time to say something. He was regarding Wolfe with narrowed eyes. "Are you saying I killed Hawthorne?"

"I seem to be hinting at that as a possibility, Mr. Davis."

"Then you're a damned idiot. And it's certainly actionable to accuse—"

"It may be. Or it may not. You're a lawyer; why don't you let me go on till I sink? Four. It is reasonable to assume that it was on Tuesday evening that Davis went to the office of his firm and, getting Hawthorne's will from the vault, typed a new first page for it—the same paper, even the same machine—and of course wording it and ending it so it would fit the continuance on the second page, where the attestations and signatures were. He would hardly have proceeded with that until Hawthorne was actually dead, though he may have done the typing previously, since it was a delicate and difficult job.

"Five. It is probable that there was no bequest to Miss Karn in Hawthorne's will. What gifts he may have made her we can only conjecture, but I doubt if her name was in his will. It isn't commonly done that way. Even if it was, the legacy was certainly a comparatively modest one. So Davis, wanting to bind Miss Karn to him with a tie that would render unlikely

further adventures with millionaires, made her a
tempting offer. If she would pledge constancy to him,
the will found in the vault would have the first page he
had typed, and she would inherit seven million dollars."

"Glenn Prescott drew the will," May Hawthorne
said acidly.

Wolfe nodded. "Yes. But six. Davis had calculated
the risk. If there was a duplicate of the will anywhere,
he knew where it was, and either destroyed it or gave
it a new first page also. There were only three other
sources of evidence of the contents of the will as
originally drawn. The stenographer's notebook. That,
following routine, had been destroyed. The stenographer herself. She also had been destroyed, by death.
Glenn Prescott, his partner, who had drawn the will.
There was his risk, and he took it. He was shrewd,
audacious, and desperate, and he took it. He knew
Prescott; he knew that the dearest thing to his heart
was the reputation and prosperity of that law firm. So
he calculated: Prescott, getting the will from the vault
and discovering the substitution that had taken place,
would be shocked, horrified, stunned. He would suspect at once that Davis had done it. But would he
expose him?"

Davis blurted in a rasping sarcastic tone, "Good
God, you were sunk long ago."

"I'm going deeper yet," said Wolfe imperturbably.
"Davis answered that question, would Prescott expose
him, with a no. Prescott regarded Davis as a rarely
gifted lawyer, the kind that makes history. He knew
he was being ruined by his infatuation for Miss Karn.
With Hawthorne dead, and Miss Karn's greediness so

adequately satisfied, thanks to Davis, Davis might have her and be himself again, to the greater glory of the firm. On the other hand, if Prescott exposed the crime, if he disclosed the facts, whether Davis's guilt was legally established or not, the thing would be a staggering blow to the prestige and standing of the firm. Dunwoodie is an old man, hardly more than a name. Prescott has ability but no brilliance, and knows it. With Davis out, and such a stink pervading that office, the firm would be ruined.

"Davis figured that was the way Prescott would react, and he was right. I don't know how long Prescott struggled with himself about it, but finally he took the will up to the Hawthorne residence on Thursday evening and read it to the family gathered there. Then, of course, he was irrevocably committed. Davis was safe as far as Prescott was concerned. But he found himself confronted by another danger. Where and how and when it first showed itself, I don't know, nor have I any proof that Naomi Karn became convinced that Davis had killed Hawthorne, and either threatened to expose him—which seems unlikely—or announced an invincible repugnance to intimate association with a murderer—which seems much more probable. At any rate, the result was that when Davis entered the Hawthorne living room yesterday afternoon and saw Miss Karn there, he knocked her on the head and strangled her and shoved her behind—Archie!"

I was out of my chair, but I wasn't needed. Davis had jerked himself up, halfway to his feet, and Cramer had thrust out an arm to block him, but even that hadn't been necessary. He had made an inarticulate noise of pain, no words, and dropped back again as if it was too much for him. He flopped there limp, staring at Wolfe.

Wolfe looked not at Davis, but at his partner, and went on: "Now, Mr. Prescott, it's up to you. I have a couple of items of evidence, but before I present them I want an understanding with you. Your attempt to save your firm from ruin has failed. The murderer of Hawthorne and Miss Karn is going to pay for it. If you want to help us in that, this is your chance and your last one." Wolfe's eyes went to the right. "Mr. Skinner, I said I have evidence, and I have. But Mr. Prescott can help us if he feels like it. I suggest that if he gives valuable testimony for the state against a murderer, it would be appropriate not to prosecute him as an accomplice in a forgery."

Skinner growled, "That's in my discretion."

"I know it is."

"Well," Skinner looked wary. "It depends on the testimony." He eyed Prescott. "I'll say this. If you help me, I'm likely to help you. If you don't, and you concealed a forgery, God can help you."

Everybody was looking at Prescott. His face was certainly a sight. Added to the fact that it was swollen and puffed and bruised, it was now a sickly purplish tinge all over, as if the traffic in the blood vessels had got into a jam that couldn't be untangled. He wouldn't look at Davis; he wouldn't even look at Skinner because he was in Davis's direction. With one fairly decent eye and one only a slit, he regarded Wolfe and stammered:

"What—what do you want me to say?"

"The truth, sir. About the will, what—"

Davis put in sharply, "Don't be a fool, Glenn. Keep your mouth shut."

"About the will," Wolfe repeated. "Davis is done for anyway. What sum did Hawthorne will to Miss Karn?"

"He—I can't—"

"Spill it!" Skinner barked.

Prescott squeezed it out. "He left her nothing. She wasn't mentioned."

"I see. And to his wife?"

"The residue. There was—a million to each of his sisters. Bequests to servants and employees, and his niece and nephew—they weren't changed. A million to the science fund of Varney College. The residue would have been something over two million."

"Good—Archie, make a note of that and take the rest—I could badger you with a string of questions, but I'd rather not. You tell me. You're a lawyer, and you know what I want, if you've got it. What can you tell me?"

The purple tinge on Prescott's face was coming and going. He was an object. But his voice was suddenly stronger: "I can tell you—when I saw Miss Karn on Thursday—she admitted that Davis had done it and she had conspired with him. She told me all—"

"You sniveling liar!"

It was Eugene Davis, suddenly on his feet. Cramer was up too, grabbing his arm. So was I, but again I wasn't needed. Davis, making no effort at further movement, his eyes on Prescott blazing with contempt and hate, was saying it with words:

"You throw me in! You skunk! I'm sorry I beat you up! I'm sorry I touched you! You killed her! You killed her, and for old Dunwoodie's sake, for the sake of all of them down there, I smashed your face for you and that was all I was going to do! I wanted to kill you, I admit that, but I haven't got it in me to kill. I just smashed your face. And you fall into the trap this man sets for you, and you offer to throw me in! You cowardly treacherous fool!"

Davis faced Wolfe. "You're clever," he said in a cold and bitter tone. "Damned clever. And of course you're right. Prescott did it. You wanted to open me up, and you have. He wanted Naomi six years ago, but she preferred me. He has always wanted her. He's sly and he's secretive and it has gone on festering inside of him. I knew he never stopped wanting her, but I didn't know how it had rotted his insides until she told me Friday evening what he had done about the will and the proposal he had made to her. And she had accepted it. She was going to marry him. You're right about her too—she was ambitious, greedy and unscrupulous, but she—well, she's dead. When she learned Friday that Hawthorne had been murdered, she knew Prescott had killed him. To get her. And she decided to ditch him. That's why he killed her—that, and the fear that if it got hot she would squeal."

Cramer rumbled, "Sit down."

Skinner said, "Wait a minute." He was scowling at Wolfe. "You said you had evidence that Davis did it."

"No, sir. I said I had evidence. Archie, get that envelope from the safe."

I threaded my way between customers, got it and returned with it, and handed it to him. He shook the contents onto the desk, selected a snapshot, and told me to give it to Prescott. I did so. I practically had to close his fist on it, and he made no effort to look at it. His one good eye was glassy.

"That," said Wolfe, "is a picture of you, Mr. Prescott, taken at six o'clock Tuesday by Sara Dunn as you awaited her with your car in front of the shop where she works. The flower in your buttonhole is a rosa setigera. A wild rose. You remembered that yesterday and stole her camera, but you were too late. Where in the heart of New York City, where did you get that wild rose?"

He paused, but Prescott didn't reply, and obviously wasn't able to. All he could do was stare like an imbecile.

"You didn't get it in New York," Wolfe continued inexorably. "No New York florist ever has a wild rose. And when you left your office around one o'clock Tuesday, according to the observant young woman at the reception desk—what's her name, Johnny?"

"Mabel Shanks," said Johnny, louder than necessary. "But she isn't young."

"At any rate, a woman. What was Mr. Prescott wearing in his buttonhole when he left for lunch Tuesday?"

"A cornflower."

"Just so—And, Mr. Prescott, a wilted cornflower was found by Andy Dunn not far from Hawthorne's body, hanging on a rose briar. I have two proofs that that was a patch of rose briars, a picture of the scene taken by Sara Dunn Wednesday morning, and a plant in a vase upstairs, brought me by one of my men. I assume it was before you shot Hawthorne, while you were talking with him there, that, being as casual as possible until you got hold of the gun by some ruse,

you discarded your cornflower and replaced it with a
wild rose. Or possibly Hawthorne did that for you,
seeing that your cornflower was wilted. That appears
more likely. He laid the gun down to do that, and that
was your chance to pick it up. Then, with him dead, in
your frenzy to get away and return to New York as
fast as possible so as to establish an alibi by calling for
Miss Dunn, you forgot all about the rose, and you
were still wearing it when you arrived and Miss Dunn
took a picture of you. It was that picture that
betrayed—"

"Hey!"

Cramer jumped a good eight feet, right over
Skinner's legs and seized Prescott's throat with both
hands. I never saw anything more pitiful, and don't
want to. The poor sap had suddenly stuffed the
snapshot in his mouth and began chewing as fast as he
could with his sore and swollen jaw, and was trying to
gulp it down.

"Let him alone," Wolfe said curtly. "I have the film.
You can have him, Mr. Skinner. Please get him out of
here."

I felt the same way about it. Having looked at
Prescott all I cared to, I surveyed the famous Hawthorne gals and their entourage. You might have
thought we were running a matrimonial bureau, or
even something not so genteel. Andy and Celia were
wrapped around each other by the bookshelves. April
was letting Ossie enfold her in his protecting arms.
John Charles Dunn was leaning over June, kissing
her, and she had her hands up clinging to him.

May leveled her eyes at Wolfe and demanded,

"About the will. If he destroyed that first page, how are we going to establish—"

Wolfe merely glared at her.

The warrant for Wolfe's arrest as a material witness is in a drawer of my desk where I keep souvenirs.

The World of
Rex Stout

Now, for the first time ever, enjoy a peek into the life
of Nero Wolfe's creator, Rex Stout, courtesy of the
Stout Estate. Pulled from Rex Stout's own archives,
here is rarely seen, never-before published memora-
bilia. Each title in "The Rex Stout Library" will offer
an exclusive look into the life of the man who gave
Nero Wolfe life.

Where There's A Will

The original paperback cover for WHERE THERE'S
A WILL, from 1941.

A recipe worthy of Nero Wolfe! Scrambled eggs and
omelets the Rex Stout way.

REX STOUT

"..Stout at his best
..and mystery in a
Grade A package."

Books (Will Cuppy)

WHERE
THERE'S
A WILL

An Avon Book   —35 cents—   T-374   ICD

PLAIN OMELET

It is better to make two small omelets
than a large one. Beat four eggs in a bowl,
adding two tbsps of milk or cream if you
wish; I don't. Season to taste with salt
and pepper. Heat one scant tbsp. butter in
a skillet over a hot fire. When the butter
is hot but before it smokes, add the eggs
all at once. <u>Quickly</u>, with a fork, pull the
edges of the egg mass toward the center as
they thicken. The liquid part will immediately fill the vacant spaces. Repeat until
there is no more liquid but the eggs are
still very soft. Gentlypress the handle of
the skillet downward and let the omelet slide
toward it. When 1/3 of the omelet has slid
up the edge of the pan, fold it toward the xxxx
center with a spatula. Raise the handle to
slide the omelet in the opposite direction,
and when 1/3 is up the far edge hold a dish
(heated) under it. As the rim of the omelet
touches the dish, raise the handle until the
skillet is upside down. The result should be
an oval-shaped light-brown omelet.

SCRAMBLED EGGS

For a day when you have time to kill. If
your legs would prefer not to stand for forty
minutes, move the kitchen stool near the
range. Put your heaviest skillet on the
burner with the lowest possible heat after
breaking the eggs into it, arm yourself with
a spatula, and perch on the stool. Disturb
the eggs lazily with the spatula, and keep
on disturbing them, letting no speck go
undisturbed, until they are the consistency
you like. The amount of time will of course
depend on the heat. If it takes twenty minutes you will have a good dish. If it takes
forty minutes you will have a perfect dish,
but you will probably be so bored you won't
appreciate it. Let someone else eat it.